My Dark-Haired Lover from Liverpool –

The Diary of a Scouse Queen.

A Romantic Comedy By J S Fleming.

The Diary of a Scouse Queen is a bitter-sweet romantic comedy. Our unlikely hero, Jim, is a middle-aged gay guy. Quick-witted, and the master of the *double-entendre*, but very unlucky in love. When he meets Geno, an Italian businessman, will he finally have found the man of his dreams? Will Geno, and his remarkable family, lead Jim into a new life of happiness or is he destined for more heartache? Join them in their hilarious adventures as they travel from Liverpool to Rome, and back again. If you enjoy a laugh, then please have a read; especially if you have Liverpudlian connections.

A work of fiction.

For my darling Vin, my love, my light, my life;

and dedicated to all those waiting for love.

"I always say, keep a diary and someday it'll keep you." (Mae West).

Chapter 1.

Saturday 1st August 2015.

I'm so excited. Mega-excited. I met a lovely fella last night. Geno. Italian. With beautiful brown eyes and dark hair. An accent that could melt your cornetto. Very much my type. Well, let's be honest, my type is anything with a pulse and a pair of trousers. And the pulse isn't absolutely essential; you can always resuscitate them first. They're usually more grateful then. All this time I have been joking about popping out to Subway at night to pick up a foot-long Italian, and now I might have actually found one.

No, but Geno is stunning. From Blundellsands, if you please. And he's got prospects; a real entrepreneur. He's even got his own company car. Well, I say 'car'; it's more of a company vehicle. OK, so it's an ice cream van. But what's wrong with that? It's a steady job and some might say it takes a lot of licking.

I was taking my evening stroll along the beach at Crosby (it's usually best to get out for a bit when my medication starts to wear off), and there he was: a vision of loveliness in catering. I wouldn't normally go for an ice cream man. Knowing my luck with men, I thought I would end up with either Mr Softy (which is not much use, let's be honest) or Mr Whippy (and I'm really not into M&S). But he was gorgeous, a Latin Adonis. His chimes were ringing on the van, but, to be honest, his charm was louder.

Now subtlety is not really my thing. So I grabbed the bull by the horns and marched straight up to the van. "Can I help you with anything?" he said, the words dripping off his tongue just like his raspberry sauce. "Yes, you can rip me vest off for starters", I thought, but retaining a modicum of composure, instead I asked him for a 69. I apologised immediately and explained I really meant a 99, coyly blushing and feigning complete innocence. He had a naughty twinkle in his eye and invited me into the van. Well again, let's be honest, I'm no stranger to nipping in through the back door, so I thought 'why not?'

Inside the ice cream van, it was like watching a master artist at work. Geno was hard at work making the most wonderful sundaes (I don't know why, 'cos it was Friday). He was putting in fab ingredients: sherry, jelly, custard and cream. I said, "Oh Geno, I do hope you're not trifling with my affections!". He didn't laugh. Mind you, looking at that bronzed god, I think he's the trifle. Yes, I bet he's had hundreds and thousands on top of him.

But his kiss was lovely. I felt so safe in his strong arms. I can't sleep for thinking about him, so I'm up writing my diary. The image of nibbling on his sponge fingers is still emblazoned on my mind. Well, I've sucked on worse over the years, let's be honest. Yes, I think I could get used to having an ice cream man around the place. Well, it's better than when I was dating Steve from Sayer's bakery; with him, all I got was crusty bloomers.

Sunday 2nd August 2015.

That Geno is so forward. You know he hasn't so much as taken me for a drink or taken me to the pictures yet. Nothing. But he's right in there asking for a kiss and cuddle. We were sat together downstairs and he suggested we pop upstairs for a quick kiss and hug. So we went upstairs and had a little cuddle. It was only then I realised we were still on the X2 bus going back to Crosby. I was proper mortified. Oh well, perhaps it's a good sign that he will always invite me to go riding on top. I just hope he's gentle when he punches my ticket.

And he's so suggestive. And me a good Catholic boy. I didn't know where to look. There he was, bold as brass, inviting me to have a screw as Waterloo. I won't tell you what he asked me to do at Burbo Bank. Perhaps he meant a screwball ice cream, but then I dread to think what he's using for the gobstoppers. No, I'm not looking forward to my next confession. I've got a feeling that ten Hail Mary's aren't going to cut it.

Geno can't see me tonight as he's going to the gym to get toned up. As if he needs to. I said "Oh Geno, I was hoping that I might be the Jim to get you all hot and sweaty". He managed a little chuckle this time. I mean I would have offered to go with him, but I'm not sure that they'd let me in after that little misunderstanding in the steam room. Something about an instructor saying I had to wear a towel. Well, 'towel' and 'scowl' sound so similar, don't they? Especially when you're all steamed up. Still, it did my sinuses no end of good.

No, try as I might, I didn't have much luck at the gym. You go in hoping for a six-pack, but come out with a 24 pack, buy-one-get-one-free. So he's there busy pumping iron. I wish he was here busy pumping me.

Never mind, hopefully I'll see Geno tomorrow. I'll have to stay in tonight. Maybe watch a little telly. You know, fellas are like tellies, aren't they? You can sit there and twiddle the knob all night long, but still the picture doesn't get any better. Still, with Geno, the picture is perfect.

Monday 3rd August 2015.

I went round to Geno's tonight for coffee after work. He's got a lovely little flat in Blundellsands. He's so talented, not just with ice cream, but with coffee too it seems. A proper baptista. Or is it barista? I get confused with words like that. Still I hope he is a proper back twister later! You should have seen him in the kitchen - he can grind my beans any time. And when his nozzle started frothing, I didn't know where to put myself. "Oh Geno", I said, "Coffee, sounds wonderful. I like to have something hot inside me."

Geno says that coffee is very important in Italy; he says coffee is like love. As hot as hell, as black as night, as sweet as love. Sounds very seductive. I'm only used to Camp Coffee but I didn't admit that to him. I was so excited when he offered me two shots - but a little disappointed when it turned out he meant this little drink. Espresso, honestly, what is that? It comes in such a tiny cup, I said I'd better have 4. After my third, I vaguely remember being on the ceiling, dusting I think.

And Geno has this beautiful cat, called Clara. She's a lovely grey and white colour and so friendly. It was nice to be snuggled up on the couch, wrapped up safely in Geno's arms; Clara purring away. I do appreciate that it is a bit unorthodox for a gay man to spend his evening stroking pussies, but I think you have to keep an open mind about these things.

Geno's kiss was as hot as hell and as sweet as love. But it didn't go further than that. He's one of those 'gentlemen'; he wants to wait. I mean I want to wait too, for about half an hour or so, so I have the chance to take me coat off. Oh well, patience is a virtue, I suppose.

Tuesday 4th August 2015.

Geno invited me around again this evening after work. He said he had something special to show me. Something large. Something we could play with together. I was a bit taken aback when it turned out to be a massive telly stuck on the wall. "That's nice" I said. He said he was going to hook up this X box thing to it so we could have a bit of a fiddle with it. Well, that sounded a bit more promising, but I must admit I wasn't very familiar with all this technology.

When Geno said he wanted COD, I thought "OK" and dutifully trotted off to the chip shop. It turned out that COD stood for 'Call of Duty - Black Socks', some sort of video game. I was mortified, I hadn't seen anything like it. There was this zombie bus driver driving a bus. There were guns everywhere; honestly, the windows were blown in, the roof was ripped off the bus. It was just like a Friday night on the 10A.

I said "Geno, it's great that you are so good with your hands, but surely we could find something else to twiddle with?". He smiled and asked if I would like to see his bedroom. Things were looking up! Or so I thought. When he opened the door to the bedroom, all I could see was clothes strewn on the floor. "Who's he had in here?" I thought, but he just apologised that he hadn't had a chance to tidy up. So of course I offered to help and got down on the floor. I soon had the clean clothes folded and put away, and the others in the laundry basket. Typical. I really wanted to spend my evening on my hands and knees in a young man's bedroom, but this wasn't really what I had in mind. But he thanked me, and kissed me, and held me in his strong arms. I felt his hot Latin breath as he nibbled at my ear. I felt sure he was going to whisper something romantic in my ear. "Jim?", he said. "Yes baby?", I replied. "Do you know how to use a microwave?".

Hmm, I get the feeling this lad needs a mother rather than a boyfriend. I wonder if we have a future together? I hope so; I really like him. Perhaps I could mother him first and then smother him later?

Wednesday 5th August 2015.

Oh, why haven't I heard from Geno? It's been nearly eighteen hours since I last saw him. Not a text. Nothing. What have I done wrong? Why would he be upset with me? I hope I haven't blown it. Before I've even had a chance to blow it. Is it an Italian thing? Mind you, knowing that lad he's probably put his mobile into the microwave or the washing machine. Or perhaps he's mixed up his phone with the TV remote. I can just see him now, trying to change channels with his mobile, stabbing away at the buttons. That'll learn him when he gets a phone bill for £3000.

Well, I don't care. I'm a confident, independent guy. I don't need some man to complete me. But I miss him. I miss his smile, his kiss, his arms.

Oh, I'm just being daft; he's probably just busy. I bet he's dreaming up some fabulous new ice cream desserts for his menu. I should take a leaf out of his book and spice up my career. I really fancy becoming a binman. I get so jealous of the bin lorries when I see their big signs on the front - 'Caution-Men working at the rear'.

Maybe he doesn't want me. Maybe I should find myself a new man. I believe that Tom Daley likes older men. Well, let's be honest, I'd settle for Tom Fortnightly, never mind Tom Daley.

I think I'll have an early night. Well, I'll just check my phone one last time, in case I've missed a message.

Thursday 6th August 2015.

I couldn't take it anymore. So I went round to Geno's flat. No reply. The door was locked but I put my lock-picking skills to good use and fiddled round with a hair pin until I managed to open the door. I felt like Goldilocks breaking into a maisonette to nick a bit of porridge.

Inside, there was no sign of Geno, but on further investigation I discovered some strange sounds coming from the bedroom. I threw open the door and there found Geno, bold as brass, with another fella.

He said "It doesn't mean anything. He's just an escort". "Escort indeed!", I said, "Don't be ridiculous! Everybody knows that Ford's stopped making escorts years ago!" If anything, he looked more like a convertible, 'cos it looked like he got his top off quick enough.

"No", said Geno, "an escort is someone you pay to, well, to keep you company". "What?!", I thought. Yeah, it didn't look like they were playing Scrabble over a mug of Horlicks. Well, if they were, they must take shuffling the letters very seriously, the way that duvet was moving. It's disgusting. It's immoral. I wonder what he charges?

The 'escort', looking rather sheepish, got dressed and left. Well, I suppose I could see what Geno saw in him. He was another Latin stunner. Tall, dark and handsome, with rock hard buttocks that looked like two hard-boiled eggs rolling around in a handkerchief. One of my exes said my bum was like two eggs in a hanky, but I think he meant they were scrambled. They certainly weren't soft boiled, 'cos he never dipped his soldiers in, no matter how much I begged.

"Oh Geno", I said, "If you were lonely, why didn't you call me? You don't have to be alone". He just gave me that cheeky smile of his, expecting to be forgiven. But how could I be angry at a face like that?

Friday 7th August 2015.

Geno wants to make it up to me. He's got a big night out planned for Saturday night. And I get the feeling that he's going to ask me to stay over. So I thought I'd better get organised, just in case, with a little visit to Boots. Not shoplifting, no, those days are behind me. I've still not recovered from the time I nicked that frozen chicken from Iceland. Believe me, it's no fun waiting half an hour for a bus with a frozen chicken up your jumper. I ended up in Whiston Hospital with hypothermia. And you should have seen the state of my giblets. I don't even know why I nicked a chicken. Being vegetarian, I don't eat meat. But I do like to suck on it occasionally. The worst part was when the magistrate said I had to do community service in a cooker factory, which explains my current career. No, if it ever happens again, I'm going to pay the fine. But hopefully I won't be tempted to thieve again. It can be very difficult being a gay ex-shoplifter; it makes it very hard to go straight.

So I went into Boots looking for a bit of rejuvenation. One of the make-up girls came running over and asked if I'd like to try the Elizabeth Arden time capsules to help restore youthful vitality. I said "Thank you, but I think the only time capsule that could help me regain youthful vitality now is the flippin' Tardis". So instead I plonked myself in front of the Clinique counter to try a bit of skincare and slap.

I love going to the Clinique counter. The girls always remind me of gay daleks, you know 'Ex-fo-li-ate!'. Have you ever looked in a mirror, then wished you hadn't? Especially when you're sat in the middle of Boots with one of those silver spotlights on you, and they've taken every bit of slap off you. Still, I've got to hand it to those Clinique girls. They really know how to work miracles. A little cream and powder and I was looking human again. A spray of cologne and I was good to go.

Before leaving Boots, I thought that it would be a good idea to pick up some protection. Well, you can't be too careful now can you? Things have really changed since I was younger. The choice is baffling. Do you want to be smooth and sensuous? Do you want to be thick and long-lasting? Do you want to be ribbed and studded with excitement? Honestly, why can't they just make one that says 'perfect for slappers who like a shag'? It would be so much simpler.

And don't get me started on those squirty lubricants! How can you choose between tingly mint, fruity apple and luscious strawberry? It's like flippin' harvest festival in there. In my day we didn't have squirty lubricants. Well apart from WD40. Still, at least nothing squeaked back then.

I was shattered after my trip to Boots, so I went home for a little lie down. It's not easy being gorgeous at my age, you know. It takes it out of you. I just hope that Geno can put it back in me ;)

Saturday 8th August 2015.

Oh my goodness; tonight's the night!! I'm so excited. I'm meeting Geno at eight. I will tell you all about it later. For now, I need to make myself look gorgeous. It may take a while...

****

So, we arranged to meet at 8 o'clock, under the clock at Lime Street station. So romantic. And handy. I'm usually down Lime Street most nights - not necessarily catching the train. I checked my appearance in the mirror, sprayed on a little more cologne, and headed out to get the bus into town. I was so excited when the bus came along, it's destination board proclaiming that it was going to Mann Island. To be honest, I was a bit disappointed when I discovered it only meant that it was going to the Pier Head. I've a good mind to report them to Merseytravel; they'll get done under the Trades' Descriptions Act.

The journey just flew by and I was in town before I knew it. I walked over to Lime Street and into the station. The main concourse was full of people, but there, underneath the clock, I spotted a lean, tall man, with jet black hair. As I got closer, he flashed me a beautiful smile. His brown eyes seemed to light up as he wrapped me in his arms and kissed me.

"So, am I forgiven?" asked Geno. "We'll see", I said, trying to play hard to get, "But you may have to do penance later", I teased. Penance? Who am I kidding? It's usually me who ends up on his knees by the end of the evening. And knowing my luck, if I asked him to pray the rosary for a penance I'd end up getting stuck on the sorrowful mysteries. "So", I asked, "what do you have planned for this evening?". "It's a surprise, a little treat", he said, and he took my hand and led me, blissfully happy, out of the station and through the streets.

We had a lovely stroll through town, chatting and catching up. I loved hearing about all the cute things that Clara had been doing - a boy's best friend is his pussy after all. We stopped by Liverpool One, just outside Debenhams. Then panic set in. Why had he brought me to the shops twenty minutes after closing time? Had he heard about my former penchant for breaking and entering into retail establishments - usually followed by robbing them blind? Who had been talking? But luckily, that wasn't his intention. All became clear when the Tuk Tuk pulled up. I had seen the Tuk Tuks driving around town, of course, and thought they looked like great fun, but had never been in one. And this one was the Karaoke Tuk Tuk. I couldn't believe that he had gone to all this trouble and made special arrangements to get the Karaoke Tuk Tuk just for me.

"Thank you Geno", I said, "How did you know that I liked karaoke?" "Oh, just a hunch, you know. You're always singing, and then there's that huge Abba music collection on your phone". Oh my goodness, I wonder what else he has seen on my phone?! "So Geno", I asked, "have you been on the Tuk Tuks before?". "No baby", he replied softly, "I wanted my first time to be with you". Well, I've heard that line before, but still my heart melted. To be honest, I was relieved to find that there was something left in the city that he hadn't ridden on yet.

We stepped into the Tuk Tuk, the lights and music started up, and we were off! It was so magical to be travelling around town, cuddled up to Geno, singing along. I was a bit embarrassed when Geno started singing along to One Erection. He couldn't quite get the words right. "So tell me boy if every time we to-o-ouch, you get this kind of ra-aash" and "if you don't wanna take it slow, and you just wanna fill my hole, then baby say yeah yeah yeah yeah". A bit common, I thought; but I'll let him off. He's not a native English speaker after all.

When the Tuk Tuk finally came to a stop and it was time to step off, I kissed Geno and thanked him for a lovely ride. I hoped it wouldn't be the last time I got to say that. Geno asked if we should go for a little bit of dinner. "Wonderful", I said, "I knew I could rely on you for a little nibble, Geno".

At the restaurant, Geno treated me to all the finest Italian delicacies. I was a bit unsure about the stuffed mushrooms. Well they don't sound so appetising when they describe them as *'funghi'*, do they? Still, I have had worse things in my mouth, let's be honest. I suspect Geno has a mushroom that I wouldn't mind stuffing.

I was so happy travelling back to Blundellsands, snuggled up with Geno, gazing into his eyes. When we got to his flat, we had a lovely smooch on the sofa. Then he suggested that we might be more comfortable in the bedroom. Again, that's a line that I've heard before, but I didn't mind. It was so wonderful to be cuddled up with Geno in bed. Clara insisted on jumping up on the bed and snuggling down. Not quite the type of threesome I am used to, but there you go. I kissed Geno deeply and opened my arms to receive his love. I said 'I opened my arms'. Honestly, dirty ticket.

Sunday 9th August 2015.

Oh, I'm shattered. Geno has had me on my hands and knees all night. Mind you, the cooker did need a good clean. I can see now why they say that Italians have Roman hands. Oh, that lad is wild. He pops two Viagra and thinks he's Mussolini. But he's so sweet. I remember once

I got a bit confused and asked the doctor for 'Niagara' by mistake. I couldn't stop weeing for days.

Geno kissed me 'good morning'. He said he hoped that he hadn't woken me too early. Oh no, I live right up in the north of the county, almost in the countryside, so I'm used to being aroused by a persistent cock in the mornings. It keeps crowing and crowing. As opposed to Geno's, which keeps growing and growing. I loved snuggling up with him.

Geno asked me if I'd like something hot and steamy (of course I did!) but he meant a shower and a coffee. After showering, he went into the kitchen to prepare the coffees, and while he was busy there playing with his nozzle, I went to sit in the living room, with Clara on my lap. I heard a buzz and saw Geno's phone flash into life. A picture of a stunning guy with dark features popped up on the screen along with the name 'Rafaella'. A message popped up saying 'Can't wait to see you soon'. As Geno came into the living room, I passed him his phone and asked, "Geno, baby, who is Rafaella?". "Oh, it's nothing", he replied. I wasn't reassured, and looked at him hoping for more of an explanation. "What?", he said; "What are you inseminating?"

Chapter 2.

Wednesday 12th August 2015.

It's been a few days since I asked Geno about Rafaella. He hasn't said any more about it. I don't know what is going on. I mean, Geno says he still likes me. Let's be honest, the nice guys I meet always say that they like me; generally just not enough to shag me or to be seen with me in public. I really hoped that Geno was going to be different.

And the strangest thing is that Geno wants me to meet Rafaella! Why would he want that? Why would I want to go and meet his bit on the side? Why would I want to meet a stunning, dark, handsome Italian stallion? Oh, who am I kidding? Of course I want to see Rafaella. Curiosity always killed the cat. I must remember not to say that in front of Clara.

Is Geno thinking of having one of those threesomes that people keep talking about? I think it's called a *ménage a trois*. I couldn't manage an *un* never mind a *trois*! I don't think I could handle two randy Italians (although it might be fun to try). Knowing my luck, I'd be hoping for a salami, but I'd end up with a chipolata. No, there is no way I'm tying up two handsome Italians and licking tiramisu off them. I don't care what they're paying. It's got very hot and stuffy in here all of a sudden.

Or maybe Geno is thinking about having us both as partners. Like a foreman. Or is it a Mormon? Mind you, that's just being greedy, having two fellas. Goodness knows, I'd settle for one. Though I suppose it would be better to share Geno than to not have him at all. Geno has got a lot to offer a guy, so I suppose I can't keep him all to myself. Perhaps he wants to see other people and have an open relationship. Well, I've had open relationships before; you know, when you're hopin' that they'll sling their hook before too long.

Oh well, I'll just have to see how it goes. I'm meeting Rafaella tomorrow. I'll try to be calm and dignified. You know me, the soul of disinfection.

Thursday 13th August 2015.

So, Geno and I went down to Lime Street at 6 p.m. to meet Rafaella. He was getting the train over from Manchester Airport, having flown in from Rome apparently. I would love to visit Rome someday. I'd love to see the Vatican and Saint Peter's Brazilian, and kiss the Pope's ring. Geno was all cock-a-hoop (no pun intended). "I can't wait to see Rafaella", he said, "He's such a great guy". "Oh, I'm sure", I hissed. "Yes", Geno continued, "and he's so talented in the kitchen. You should see his dough balls". "Way too much information", I said. "And he'd better behave himself", I continued, "otherwise I'll be chopping his dough balls off and wearing them as earrings on Saturday night!"

"Don't be like that, Jim. Rafaella is really nice", Geno went on, singing his praises. "And he's really brave. He works as a fireman, you know". "Oh, you've got to be careful with firemen, Geno", I warned; "I mean, he might have a big hose, but he'll be spraying it everywhere. It might be fun to get a fireman's lift, but when they ask you to slide down their fireman's pole, well, it's just a step too far". "Behave yourself", Geno said. "Look, the train is pulling in".

I braced myself ready for the arrival of Rafaella. Amidst the crowds getting off the train, I saw this beautiful tall man; flawless olive skin;

jet black hair; piercing brown eyes; a gleaming smile. I prayed to God that he wasn't Rafaella, but of course he was; I recognised him from the photo on Geno's phone. I tried so hard to hate him, but it was so difficult; he was lovely. Geno stepped forward and greeted Rafaella with a hug and a kiss on both cheeks. "You look great", said Geno, "that is a beautiful shirt". "What, this old thing?", Rafaella replied, "I just threw it on". "And missed", I muttered. Geno ignored me and carried on. "It looks like you've been working out", Geno complimented Rafaella. "Oh yes, I've been working on my bubble butt". "Well, just be careful you don't get a prick in your bubble butt, or that bubble will burst!", I said, seething with resentment. Geno gave me a glance, instructing me to be nice. Honestly, bubble butt indeed! What's the point of having a round bum? You can't sit down without falling over.

"So", Rafaella asked Geno, "who is your friend, Geno?" "This is Jim", said Geno, introducing me. I did my best to smile. "And Jim", Geno continued, "please meet Rafaella, *mio fratello*." "Who the hell is 'Mia'?", I asked. "I thought his name was Rafaella?" "Oh Jim", said Geno, "'*mio fratello*', it means 'my brother'." The penny dropped. That swine; he had me worried all this time, and the hot Latin hunk was his brother. "But Geno, why didn't you tell me that it was your brother who was coming?", I questioned. "I'm sorry, baby. I couldn't resist teasing you", Geno replied; "Am I forgiven?". "We'll see", I said, pretending to be annoyed. "Let's take Rafaella to see a bit of the city if he's not too tired".

So we all went for a little walk around the city, and had a little stroll around the Pier Head and looked at the Three Graces. "The waterfront is beautiful", said Rafaella. "Did you come down when the Three Queens visited the river?" "Yes I did", I answered, "but to be honest, when I'm out on a Saturday night there are usually hundreds of queens in town, so three queens at the Pier Head was not such a big deal".

Friday 14th August 2015.

Geno phoned me at lunch time. He said he had only had a Snickers bar for lunch. "Well that's nice," I said, "I'm glad I'm not the only one who likes to nibble nuts". He said he didn't want to spoil his appetite because he was going to dinner with Rafaella, and asked if I would like to join them. "Oh lovely, Geno", I said, "I can always rely on you for a little nibble".

I met them in town after work, and Geno led us to this beautiful Italian pizzeria. "Is this pizzeria OK for you?", Geno asked. "Oh yes", I replied, "I like a nice pizzeria. Well it makes a change from having the gonorrhoea, let's be honest".

Inside, there were lots of lovely authentic Italian touches. I especially liked the long wooden pepper mills. "I wonder if they'd notice if I nicked one?", I thought. They were just the thing to keep handy to belt a fella if he tried any funny business.

We sat down, and Geno seemed to be even more stunning in the candle-light, as did his brother. I was keen to learn more about Rafaella, so I asked him about his work. "Rafaella, you are so brave being a fireman. Don't you get scared when you have to rescue people from burning buildings?" "Well no, not really," he replied, "We get trained and we have all the equipment. I usually find it easier to have the guy on top. I throw him over my shoulder and take him out". "Oh Rafaella", I mused, "we have so much in common".

Then he asked me if I had ever thought of joining the fire brigade. "Not really", I said, "I don't really feel like a young man any more (although I certainly would like to feel a young man), and I'm not so keen on driving. I don't know how I'd be driving a fire engine". It's true, I really don't enjoy driving and haven't driven for a while. It took me a couple of attempts to pass my driving test. I remember my first driving instructor who exclaimed with frustration: "Well Jim, at least when you buy your first car you'll be able to save a bit of money on it!". "Why's that?", I asked. "Well", he replied, "you'll only need about two gears, and I wouldn't bother with any mirrors if I were you!" I was proper mortified.

But Rafaella encouraged me. "I think you'd make a good fire-fighter", he said, "I'm sure you could tug on a long hose quickly". "Well", I replied, "perhaps I have got some relevant experience in that regard".

Rafaella then asked me about my work. "Oh, I'm just a technical guy involved with fixing cookers", I explained. "It keeps me very busy, though. In fact I'm so busy that the boss had to ask everyone to stop coming over to me and asking me questions. That's a shame really, 'cos I quite like guys coming over and interfering with me".

The waiter came over and took our orders. Geno recommended all the best Italian dishes. To be honest, I think I've already met the tastiest Italian dishes ;). When the first course arrived, it was such a delight to see Geno and his brother negotiating unusually large meatballs. This sight stirred rather vivid feelings inside me. "You like my meaty-balls?", asked Rafaella. "Very much indeed", I replied, in a bit of a daze. "I mean, you like to try and nibble on my meaty-balls?", he explained. "Yes! What?", I said, then finally understood what he was getting at. "Oh, I see what you mean", I said. "No, thank you. I'm a vegetarian. I'm not used to handling meat". Then Geno piped up:

"I could say something about that remark. But I'm too much of a gentleman".

As the meal went on, I asked Geno and his brother about their family. "So tell me", I asked, "do you have any other brothers or sisters?". "Yes", Rafaella said, "there are five of us altogether: Antonio, Dario, Serena, Geno and me. And of course, you should see my little Cappuccino". "Oh, Rafaella", I blushed, "I've only just met you and you want to show me your little Cappuccino?!" "That's his dog", Geno explained, getting his phone out to show me a picture. "Oh, what a sweetie, how cute", I said; "I love dogs; in fact I've had quite a few dogs myself over the years".

I probed deeper: "Whereabouts in Italy do you come from?" "We live in a small town called Castel Gandolfo, just outside of Rome. You might have heard of it? It's where the Pope sometimes goes for a summer holiday", explained Rafaella. "Yes of course", I said, "it sounds lovely". "In fact", Rafaella continued, "Antonio and Serena work for the Holy Father. Antonio serves in the Vatican police corps and Serena is a cook at the Vatican". "Wow", I said, "that's amazing working for the Holy Father. Although, I must admit, I'm more interested in your Hole-y Brother!". "Tell me what it's like at the Vatican. Is it true that the nuns have dirty habits?"

"And what made you decide to come to England?", I asked Geno. "Well, you know", he replied, "I had a successful ice cream business in Rome, and I thought that maybe the English people would like to suck on a Roman lolly". "Yes Geno", I said, "I think you may have a good point there. And if you ever need me to help with any market research, I'd be more than happy to oblige".

As the waiter cleared away the plates, Geno asked me if I had a couple of quid in change on me for the tip. "Don't be daft", I replied, "Everyone knows that queens don't carry money".

The waiter asked if we would like any desserts. Rafaella said, "No thank you, I'm watching my figure". "Believe me, mate", I said to Rafaella, "we're all watching your figure".

It was a really lovely evening. I was really falling in love with Geno and warming to his lovely brother. My heart stirred. Well, not just my heart to be honest. It was just a shame that, as the evening was drawing to a close, it started to get a bit rowdy at the bar. This small group of lads started shoving each other and started to fight. I couldn't stand it so I went over and said, "Look, it's a Friday night, lads. You should be enjoying yourselves. Nothing's worth fighting over". I had to grab one lad's arms as he was about to punch another guy. I brought his hands to behind his back until he had calmed down. "That was brave of you", Geno said. "Don't be soft", I replied, "it's just some young lads being daft. Mind you, I'm a bit out of practise. It's been a long time since I've pulled a lad off like that".

Saturday 15th August 2015.

I was enjoying a relaxing morning; glad to be having a day off for a change. Geno phoned me and asked if I would like to try something wet and wild this afternoon. My ears pricked up. Well, again, not just my ears to be honest. He said perhaps we could try some new positions and see how we got on. I nearly exploded with excitement. It's fair to say I was a bit disappointed when I found out that he meant spending the afternoon at Bootle baths with Rafaella and me.

Mind you, I love swimming, me. And Bootle baths holds a special place in my heart because it was there that I first learnt to swim. (I was 35 at the time). Swimming is such good exercise. And, of course, I love seeing hunks in trunks. (It's the weirdoes in Speedos that you've got to watch out for).

So I went to meet Geno and Rafaella, and we all went down to Bootle. We got changed and went over towards the poolside. I couldn't take my eyes off Geno and Rafaella, standing there with their dark skin and rippling muscles. My goggles steamed right up. Geno must have caught me staring at him, and he said, "So you like what you see?". "Very much so, Geno", I replied, "You look so hot standing there. And I couldn't help noticing you have a great, er, package". "Thanks Jim", said Geno, "and you look great in your trunks, too. What is it they call them over here? Bugle smotherers?". "Budgie smugglers", I gently corrected him, "and thank you, love, but it certainly doesn't look like I'm smuggling a budgie, I'm afraid. Possibly an earthworm".

"Excuse me", said Rafaella, "but if I could interrupt you two love birds for a moment, I think we are missing all the fun in the water". I apologised and we walked closer to the pool. It was then that panic struck me, and I shrieked, "I am not going in that! Not at my time of life. No way am I going in that!" "What's the matter, baby?", Geno asked. "Are you afraid of the water slide?" "No", I said, "not the slide. It's the toddler's paddling pool that freaks me out!" Well, the way the water tickles your feet in that thing can be really unsettling, you know? "Don't worry, baby", said Geno, "we'll just have a swim in the main pool". So we did.

I enjoyed doing my laps up and down the pool. But really it was Geno's beauty that I was lapping up. He looked stunning, and so graceful and strong in the water. Thank God for goggles with prescription lenses, that's all I can say. They have really transformed my life. Now I can see everything. Geno said, "You're a really good swimmer now, Jim. Come on, let's see your different positions. Let's see how you do on your back. Let's see how you look on your front". My goodness, if I had a pound for every time I've heard those lines, I wouldn't have to work at all.

But I enjoyed the rest of my swim; I love the weightless feeling as you go through the water. It's cold when you get out, of course, but then there are the warm showers to perk you up. It's nice to have the warm water caressing your skin. Of course, I wish it was Geno caressing my skin in the shower. Well, I wish he'd get his loofah out, to be honest. Oh well, maybe we'll get the chance to be together soon.

Sunday 16th August 2015.

Oh, I woke up with a shocking cold. I think I must have caught a chill at the baths. I've been coughing shocking. It's definitely time to suck a fisherman's friend. It's always a bit embarrassing, though, when the fisherman complains. Perhaps that's why they won't let me go down to the marina anymore?

I always seem to be getting the snuffles. Especially when it is raining on the way into work. Talk about getting pissed on at Whiston.

Geno has asked me to go down to Lime Street with him this afternoon to see Rafaella off. It seems he has to fly back to Rome tonight because he is due back at work in a couple of days. I suppose all good things must come to an end.

****

Geno and I took Rafaella down to Lime Street station at about 3 p.m. I had really liked meeting Rafaella and was very sorry to see him go. "Do you have to go back to Italy so soon?", I asked. "Oh yes", he replied, "These fires won't put themselves out, I'm afraid. I have to be back at the fire station on Tuesday. I don't want to be late and get into trouble with the boss!" "Oh no", I agreed, "You certainly don't want to get into trouble with your boss. I mean, I know what it's like when you have a fella on your back giving you a hard time".

Rafaella smiled and hugged me. "It was good to meet you, Jim", he said; "Perhaps you could come over to Rome and see us all sometime? I would love to see more of you". "Thanks, but I'm afraid I've got nothing else worth seeing!", I replied. It's true, I'm not much to look at. Perhaps I should have some of that cosmetic surgery that people are talking about. I could certainly do with a few enhancements. Then again, perhaps I shouldn't meddle with what the good Lord gave me. Mind you, what the good Lord gave me isn't worth meddling with, let's be honest.

Geno and I both kissed and hugged Rafaella as he got on the train back to the airport. We waved as the train pulled away, and then I turned to Geno and hugged him. "I'm sorry baby", I said, "you must be sad to see your brother go". "Yes", Geno replied, "but hopefully I will see him again soon, probably next year. He has to go and be a hero; he has to go and put his fires out". "Yes", I said, "he's a fine fireman. But I think there is one fire that he couldn't put out". "What's that?", Geno asked. "The fire you have started in my heart", I said, and leant in to kiss him. (Well, we're all allowed a cheesy line every now and then. Italians like cheese, don't they?).

"I think you might be lonely tonight, Geno, without your brother", I said. "I'd love to go home with you, hold you in my arms, and keep you company". (Well, if you don't ask, you don't get, do you?). "I'd really like that, Jim", Geno replied, and we left the station, arm in arm, to get the bus back to Crosby.

Later, curled up with Geno on his sofa, I couldn't have been happier. "This sofa is so comfy", I said. "Yes, of course", explained Geno, "it is pure bliss when you sit on a solid Italian construction like this". Hmm, my sentiments exactly!

We kissed and cuddled, and I fell in love with Geno a little more. Then he said, rather ominously, "Jim, I'm sorry; I have something to tell you". I felt a crushing feeling come over me (not in a good way), and thought "Typical. This is just my luck". "I have to go away for a while", Geno continued. "Oh Geno, no", I protested; "Why? You're not wanted by the police are you? I was really hoping that I might be the only man who wanted you".

Chapter 3.

Tuesday 18th August 2015.

I was worried about Geno, and wondered why he had to go away. Isn't it just my luck to find a great guy and then to lose him? Or frighten him off. What had I done to push him away? I certainly didn't want to push him off. Quite the opposite in fact. I really needed to talk to him, so I popped round to his flat after work.

Geno answered the door in his boxers. Yes, I know it's a strange place to have a door, but very convenient. I think it was marked 'tradesman's entrance'. "Jim", he said, "how nice of you to pop up". "We usually say 'pop in'", I explained, "but I'll pop up for you, mate, any time you like". I could see that Geno had been pressing his bits. "Do you need anything ironing, while I have the iron out?", he asked. "Only my face, to be honest", I replied.

"Geno", I said, "I'll come straight to the point". "That's not like you", he said. "Very funny", I continued, "Geno, I just don't get it. (Well, not as often as I'd like to anyway). Why do you have to go away? I thought we liked each other?" "Of course I like you, Jim", he explained, "it's just that I need to grow...". "No, Geno", I interrupted, "You don't need to grow any more. You're quite big enough, thank you very much". "I mean I need to grow my business", Geno went on, and he explained his plans to me.

After Geno had explained things, I tried to clarify his plans. "So, let me get this straight, you have to go to Skegness for 9 days for the National Union of Ice Cream Workers' Annual Conference. The theme this year is 'Creating a luscious lickable lolly for the modern age'?". "Yes, that's right, Jim", Geno replied, "It could be a really good opportunity for me to meet some very influential people in the industry. We get to share ideas and recipes". "Well, I hope that's all you'll be sharing", I said. "Yes of course, Jim", Geno replied, "I'll be saving my love for you".

"Oh baby", I said, "I will really miss you. When do you have to leave?". "Well I need to leave on Thursday to travel over to Skegness, and I should be back on Friday night, the following week", Geno explained. "Wow, nine days", I said, "I'll miss you, and I'll pray for you. I'll have enough days to pray a novena for a safe and successful trip". "Do you pray often?", Geno asked. "Oh yes", I replied, "You know me. I'm always on my knees".

I understood why Geno had to go. I was so proud of him. "It's wonderful that you are getting out and trying to better yourself. You're a hard worker like me. I've had to claw my way up the ladder, you know. I haven't always had a glamorous life fixing cookers". Indeed, it's tough at the top. Mind you, it's quite tough at the bottom too. And I went on to tell Geno more about my earlier life.

I'll never forget my first flat behind the Strand, just by the Territorials. My goodness, you needed the Territorials for protection sometimes. I was very happy there, but, my goodness, I knew poverty, sharing with the rats. The ice cream man that came round certainly wasn't as nice as Geno. He seemed to be selling all sorts of powders, and I don't think they were sherbet. And I had no washing machine. Every Sunday, I walked with the laundry down to the 'Clean As You Like' launderette. I was very fond of Sharon there, who worked hard ironing and sorting out the dry cleaning. I always used to save up my 20 pence pieces for her during the week so that she'd have plenty of change for the punters. In return, she'd let me jump the queue for the spin dryers. Well, you know, it is important to have a spin before you have a tumble.

"Well", said Geno, "you can always have a spin and tumble with me anytime you like. And hopefully we are heading for a brighter future. Ice cream is definitely the way forward!". "Yes, I hope so", I said. "Will you do me a favour while I'm away?", Geno asked. "Anything, baby", I said. "Could you pop in and feed Clara for me?". "Of course, Geno", I said, "I don't normally care for pussies, but I'll certainly give it a go". "Thank you", said Geno, "And do you think you could put the bin out on Fridays?". "No problem", I said, "Just tell me where to stick it".

"I'll really miss you, baby", said Geno; "Let's make the most of the time we have together. Why don't you spend the night, Jim?". "I'd love to", I said, and fell happily into his arms.

Wednesday 19th August 2015.

Oh, I am exhausted this morning! I've warned Geno. If he keeps wearing me out like this, I will have no option but to put in a claim for repetitive strain injury. And I wish that Geno would shave, just occasionally. Have you tried snogging a randy Italian with five-day stubble? Well, let's just say that I won't be needing my Clinique face scrub anymore.

I went into the kitchen and found Geno grilling sausages for breakfast. "Oh Geno", I said, "How interesting. I didn't know that you were a dirty sausage gobbler!". "Oh, you know me", he replied, "I'm a real magician. I can make a sausage disappear just like that!". I started going weak at the knees, so I thought I'd better grab a cup of tea to steady my nerves. Geno's kitchen is quite small and I needed to squeeze past him to get to the kettle, so I said, "Excuse me, you don't mind if I slide in at the back, do you?". "I thought you'd never ask", he replied.

"The tea bags are in the cupboard", said Geno, "I've got PG tips or Typhoid". "Oh, well, in that case, I think I'd better stick to the PG!", I said. "I wonder what PG stands for?", asked Geno. "Oh", I explained, "I think it means 'you're Pretty Gorgeous', Geno", and kissed him. He nearly dropped his sausage butty, but fortunately managed to keep hold of it. I might be a vegetarian, but I still hate to see a good sausage go to waste. "Oh Jim, don't put too much water in the kettle", Geno advised me, "it takes ages to come to the boil". "Really?", I said, "I find that surprising. With it being your kettle, I would have thought it would have been permanently on the boil".

After having a quick cup of tea, I explained that I'd better get off to work. "I'm mad busy at the moment sorting out spare parts for the cookers", I said. "Well, I've got most of them sorted. I really just need a knob and a screw now". "Perhaps I could help you with that sometime?", Geno asked. "Yes, I'm sure you could", I replied.

I asked Geno about his plans for the day. "Have you got much on, Geno?", I asked, "Although I must admit that I think I prefer you with less on!". "Well", said Geno, "I just need to stock the van up ready for the lunchtime rush on the beach. And I need to pop into the barbers for a little trim. You know, just a little wash, cut and blow-job". I blushed crimson. "Oh Geno", I said, "We really need to work on your English. I don't think you realise what you just said". "Sure I do", Geno said, "I know it should normally be a blow-dry but, well, Simon the barber has particular tastes". With that, I thought that I had better get off to work, so I kissed Geno 'goodbye', and ran for the bus.

Thursday 20th August 2015.

I ran from work as quickly as I could so that I would have time to see Geno off at Lime Street station. I ran into the station concourse and found Geno, underneath the clock of course, surrounded by several old bags. When I say 'bags', I mean luggage, not his ex-boyfriends. "Wow mate", I said, "I know you've got a big package, but do you really need all these packages?". "Oh yes", he said, "You know how it is; a boy has clothes. And I want to look my best when I'm dispensing soft whipped cream". "Yes, I bet you do", I replied.

"Geno, love", I said, "you will take care of yourself, won't you? And if you meet any cute guys, please be sensible and stay safe. I hope you have plenty of protection". "Yes", he replied, "I've got plenty of sunscreen". "You know what I mean", I said. "Oh Jim", he continued, "you know that I've only got eyes for you". "Thank you baby", I replied, "but I know sometimes it happens. You have got plenty of protection, haven't you?" It's always sensible to carry protection. I'll never forget one time I got a bit confused in the shops and asked for 'Dulux' by mistake. I wouldn't recommend dipping your bits in five litres of gloss emulsion. Mind you, the smell of white spirit proved to be a very effective deterrent, as no fella would come near me.

Geno leant in to kiss me and reassure me. We said our farewells and he boarded the train to Nottingham. Apparently it is quite a long journey to Skegness and you have to change in Nottingham. As the train pulled out, we waved and blew kisses. I even gave a little round of applause. Well, it's always nice to have a warm hand on your exit, isn't it?

Then I was all alone. As I left the station, dusk was falling and it was starting to get dark. I was left to walk the streets of Liverpool alone in the dark. Oh well, I suppose old habits die hard.

I went to catch the bus back to Crosby. I needed to pop in to Geno's flat before going home, just so I could feed the bins and put the cat out.

Friday 21st August 2015.

Geno phoned me to let me know he had arrived safely in Skegness. He said he'll try to keep in touch by text. And if I'm lucky, he might poke me on Facebook! I suppose that's the only type of poking I can expect for a while. Oh well, never mind. Geno said he's been very busy at the Conference already. He's had lots of mouthfuls. I do hope he's talking about ice cream. I'm starting to feel very jealous again. Talking of mouthfuls, I remember my mum, when I was little, saying that you should never put anything in your mouth unless you're going to eat it. I'm afraid to say I didn't listen to that advice.

It's a week now until Geno gets back. I feel weak just thinking about it. A whole week! But I'll keep myself busy and hopefully the time will fly. I went round to Geno's flat after work to feed Clara and make sure that she was OK. After I had fed her, I settled down on the sofa to stroke and pet her. I must admit I'd much rather be petting Geno, but there you go. Clara purred contentedly as I stroked her back and tickled her ears. You know, it's been an awful long time since I've had a pussy in my lap. Donkeys' years, in fact.

I turned the telly on. Geno's got a massive one. You know, I never thought I'd be sat down staring at a 42 inch-wide Bush. And it's one of those smart TVs. What you do is, you stick your dongle into the 42 inch-wide Bush, then it picks up the internet and you can watch all kinds. You get the GuyPlayer, YouLube and NetLix. Geno seems to have a lot of Swedish channels amongst his favourites. I'm not sure why.

Saturday 22nd August 2015.

Just six more days to go now until Geno gets back. I spoke to him on the phone and he's doing OK. I told him that I was missing him and praying for him. In fact, I told him that I was thinking of him last night when I was reading the Bible. "I hope it wasn't the parable of the prodigal son you were reading!", Geno asked, "Or perhaps you were reading about the Whore of Babylon?!". "No, of course not", I replied, "It just occurred to me, Geno, when I was reading the New Testament, that you must be the only thing in the world that has been in more hotel rooms than it has".

I made myself some porridge for breakfast. Well, it's the only way I'm going to get my oats, let's be honest. And Geno is always saying that I need more roughage. At least, I think that's what he said. I am trying to eat more healthily; after all, my body is a temple. An ancient ruin. No, really I think my body is a temple. I think that's why there's a queue of fellas waiting to get in it on a Friday night. Still, at least they take their shoes off before they come inside.

I could do with a bit of excitement. I wonder if I'll win the lottery tonight? Every week I pray that God will pick my balls. But nothing. I suppose I might have more chance if I bought a ticket.

Sunday 23rd August 2015.

Poor Geno has got the toothache. I said, "Love, you'll have to try to see a dentist at the walk-in centre". Mind you, from what he's told me, he's spent the last 72 hours doing nothing but eating ice cream. Surely that is enough to make anyone's teeth sensitive? "I'm a bit scared of dentists", he said. "Don't be daft", I replied, "Surely you don't mind having a little prick in your mouth?"

The poor thing. I wish I could be there to hold him and kiss it better. Only 5 more days to wait now.

Monday 24th August 2015.

Back to work today, and it's been mad busy. I've been trying to train people up on the new cookers and explain how the new roast probe works. The guys don't seem to get it. They insist on sticking their probes into their birds, even though I keep explaining that if you stick your probe into a bird it will likely catch against a bone and not get a proper temperature reading. No, you're much better sticking your probe into a meaty joint, but the guys will not agree with me. They insist that their birds want it. I don't know why.

I've been typing so much today that my fingers are tingling. It reminds me of my old flat-mate, Ron. He was quite a heavy smoker back in the day and, to save money, he went over to roll-up ciggies. My hands were red raw by the time I'd finished helping him to roll-up enough ciggies to last the week. Honestly, we had a thriving cottage industry in the front room. In the end, I suggested that he get some help to give up smoking. The nicotine patches were quite helpful – I used to stick them over his specs so that he couldn't find his lighter. Personally speaking, I never smoke. I just fume.

My mate, Ravi, gave me a lift home. He had a lovely bottle of cologne in his glove compartment. He was very kind, and gave me a squirt in his car.

I hope Geno's OK. Only 4 more days to go now.

Tuesday 25th August 2015.

Oh, my back is killing me. I think I've overdone it on the step machine. It's great exercise, though. You can work your legs up and down while pumping your arms at the same time. It reminds me a lot of Geno, to be honest. I've got to do something to build up my muscles. I'd kill to have one of Geno's protein shakes.

Geno said that he's having a good time at his Conference. Apparently they've come up with an exciting new flavour that's a sort of cross between apple and mint. It's meant to refresh your mouth while also leaving a tingling sensation on your tongue. Hmm, I wonder where he got that idea from? Obviously I'm not the only one who likes going to Boots.

Anyway, Geno says he'll give me a lick when he gets back. With any luck, he might let me try the ice cream too ;)

3 days and counting until I see my love again!!

Wednesday 26th August 2015.

My eczema has been really playing up; I'm so itchy. Surprisingly, I've run out of cream, but the doctor said he would squeeze me in after work. He's very obliging like that.

I went round to the surgery after work. The doctor said "Right Jim, take everything off for me please". "It's OK, doctor", I said, "it's really just my lower legs that are affected this time". "No, no Jim", he replied, "We must be thorough and check everywhere! Now, drop your trousers for me". Well, I've heard that line before, let's be honest, and so I did.

"My goodness , Jim", the doctor said, "it's very swollen!". "Well, what do you expect?", I thought to myself, "If you prod it and tug it like that it's bound to get swollen, isn't it?". "Now, I'm going to give you a prescription for some cream", the doctor said; "Rub it in twice a day. I'm keen to see the swelling come down". "Yes, I bet you are", I thought. "Also", said the doctor, "I want you to take something by mouth". "Not for less than fifty quid, I'm not", I thought to myself. "I'm giving you a prescription for a short course of steroid tablets", the doctor explained; "They will help reduce the inflammation and get the eczema under control. You're all done now, Jim; you can go now". "Thank you very much, doctor, I said, "but do you mind if I just get dressed first?".

Later on, I told Geno about my examination. He said I should put a complaint in about inappropriate touching and unprofessional behaviour. "Oh no", I said, "I'm not complaining. It's very rare that you find such a lovely bedside manner nowadays. And he has wonderful warm healing hands".

Only 2 days now until Geno and I will be together again!

Thursday 27th August 2015.

Geno's coming back home tomorrow night!! I really can't wait. I wanted everything to be perfect for him, so I went round to his flat after work to have a clean round and tidy up. I fed and petted Clara, then set about cleaning and tidying. I can be quite an old scrubber when I want to be.

Geno had a pile of dirty laundry in his room, so I put it in the washing machine. I tidied up his piles of books and CDs, and had a good dust round. I discovered that Geno has a very interesting collection of magazines. They were full of gorgeous men. They looked like male models. I must admit I'd really like to meet a model. I don't mean made out of Lego. The guys in the magazines looked like they must live in a very warm country; all tanned, and they only seemed to wear swim trunks. Mind you, it looked like they could do with buying the next size up. I mean, lycra is very stretchy, but there just didn't seem to be enough room to hold their, erm, credentials. I felt very sorry for the guy pictured in the centrefold; you should have seen where they stuck the staple. No, I really didn't know that Geno had such a keen interest in swimming. It looks like he gets a new magazine sent every week. I must ask him about it sometime. Maybe he enjoys phoning and writing to pen-pals? There are lots of little adverts in the back of the magazine listing people you can phone and visit if you are lonely or need company. That's nice. I wonder why they say you have to bring cash with you? Perhaps they're going shopping.

Friday 28th August 2015.

Geno's coming tonight! (Well, he comes most nights from what I've heard). After work, I ran to get over to Lime Street ready to meet Geno's train. On the way over to town, I checked the train app on my Samsung phone to see if Geno's train was on time. It's really handy to have these apps, and I do love the Android phones. Well, I thought when choosing my phone, I've already got the haemorrhoids, so I might as well have the Androids to go with them.

A very long train pulled into the platform – very apt, I thought. As the train came to a halt, the doors opened and the crowds started to pour out. I scanned through the sea of people, straining to see Geno. Then suddenly, there he was. Tall and dark. More handsome than I remembered. I ran over to him and hugged and kissed him. "Oh, I've missed you baby", said Geno; "You give great hugs". "Oh, you know me, Geno", I said, "I'm a technical guy. I'm good with my hands".

We got a trolley to put all of Geno's bags on and pushed it along the platform towards the taxis. Geno thought it best to get a taxi back to Crosby because he really hadn't been travelling light. "Blimey, Geno", I said, "what have you got in all these bags?". "Oh I picked up lots of useful stuff", he said, "All sorts of new flavoured syrups and sauces, and the latest compact automatic ice cream maker from Europe". "Wow", I said, "You have been busy". "Yes", said Geno, "it was a great trip; I just wish that you could have come with me, Jim. I was really lonely without you". "I would have liked to have gone with you, Geno", I said, "I missed you so much". "Well, we should travel together sometime", Geno suggested; "I think we'd have a ball". "I think we'd probably have four!", I joked. "No I'm serious", Geno continued; "I'd like to take you to places". "Well", I said, "you take me to heaven most nights!" Geno kissed me softly and said, "Thank you, baby, but it would be nice to maybe take you to see Hollywood". "Hollywood!?", I exclaimed; "You're joking, mate. I'd be lucky to get the bus to Halewood!". "Well", said Geno, "maybe we should start smaller. But I'd definitely like to take you to Rome sometime". "Yes", I agreed, "I'd really like that".

In the taxi on the way back to Crosby, Geno filled me in (no, not like that!) on his plans to grow his business. "I've realised what I need to do", he said; "Ice cream shouldn't just be a dessert or occasional treat. We need to offer a full range of snacks and drinks that people can enjoy at any time of the day. I want to help people get up in the morning and enjoy their day". "Sounds good, Geno", I said; "I think you'd be very good at that. After all, you're always getting me up of a morning. Tell me more".

Chapter 4.

Saturday 29th August 2015.

I woke up in Geno's flat this morning, blissfully happy. Geno was still asleep, so I snuggled up to him and gently stroked his chest. Apparently, it turned out to be a seventeenth-century tea chest from India. And there was me thinking it was from the British Home Stores. Silly me. But seriously, it was lovely to be able to cuddle up with Geno again. He smelled so gorgeous. I love the smell of that Dolce & Banana fragrance. It was so nice to have Geno back in time for the bank holiday weekend.

When Geno awoke, I kissed him 'good morning'. He is always so beautiful and serene in the mornings. Not like me. I usually wake up in a blind panic with a gob on like the wrath of God. Which tends to make things a bit awkward when Geno gets frisky in the mornings. I say, "You've got no chance, mate, I'm dead to the world. You might as well shag a flippin' blow-up doll". Geno said that he would fix some breakfast after putting some pyjama bottoms on. "Please don't bother to get dressed on my account", I said and smiled. After all, when you've got a great Italian landmark like the Leaning Tower of Pisa, you don't want to cover it up, do you?

After a brief visit to the bathroom, I joined Geno in the living room. Geno was eating a yoghurt. "Oh Geno", I said, "I see you've gone for a thick Greek. I made that mistake once. Poor old Stavros". "Would you like a yoghurt?", Geno asked; "They're very thick and creamy". "Sounds lovely", I said, "but I think I'll just grab a fun-size banana, if I may". And I reached for his fruit bowl. "Are you OK with that?", Geno asked; "Would you like me to peel it back for you?" (Well, I've certainly heard that line before, let's be honest). "You certainly can", I said, and smiled. "You know, Geno", I said, "you should really keep your bananas away from your other fruit. They say that bananas give off a gas that makes the other fruit ripen and spoil too quickly". "Well", replied Geno, "you should know all about a fruit giving off gas, Jim. I had to share a bed with you". Honestly, Geno can be so uncouth sometimes.

I really wanted to find out more about Geno's business plans. "I really need to probe him further", I thought. "So Geno", I said, "please tell me more about your plans to grow your business". "Well, I had plenty of time to think while I was in Skegness", Geno explained, "and I know that I can't just rely on the ice cream van. Summer is coming to an end and people won't want just ice cream in the colder weather. I need to branch out". "Great, Geno", I said, "What sort of things were you thinking of?" "Oh", continued Geno, "I was thinking of coffees, pastries and maybe some pasta and pizza dishes". "Wow Geno", I said, "you're so versatile! But surely you couldn't do that much cooking in the van?" "No", he said, "I need to get my nemesis".

I took a moment to try to figure out what he meant. "Surely", I ventured, "you mean you need to get your premises organised?" "Yes", Geno replied, "premises, that's it! I need somewhere that I can get hot, grind my beans and knead my dough". "Well, you're very welcome to do that at my place any time you like", I said; "Be my guest".

"Thank you", Geno said, "but I need some commercial premises. I'm thinking of opening a *gelateria* selling Italian ices, coffees, pastries, pasta and so on". "Great", I said, "whereabouts?" "Well", said Geno,

"I'm thinking glamour. I'm thinking class. I'm thinking sophistication. I'm thinking South Road, Waterloo". "Oh, lovely", I said. "In fact", Geno continued, "I made a few calls on the train coming back from Skegness yesterday, and the estate agent has an empty café to show me. We can have a look this afternoon if you like". "Wow", I said, "Just imagine *'Geno's Gelateria'*. It's so exciting!" And with that, Geno made a quick call to the estate agency to confirm the appointment, and then we got dressed ready to go out.

Geno had arranged to meet the estate agent at 1 p.m. and he took us to see a vacant café on the South Road. "So here's the public entrance on the main road", the estate agent explained, "but for unloading you'll probably find it easier to slip in round the back". "Tell me about it", I said.

The estate agent unlocked the door and we went inside. It was a bit dusty inside and looked as though it had been empty for a while, but it looked like it could be a very cosy café. The serving counter was still in place, with a small kitchen and store-room out the back. There were still some of the old tables and chairs strewn about the seating area. In fact, there were so many tables and chairs that it reminded me of that time I went speed dating in Birkenhead. The problem with speed dating, though, is that once everyone has taken speed, you can't remember who you've spoken to. Very confusing. Some of the tables and chairs were broken. In fact it looked a bit like an explosion in an Ikea factory. But nothing that we couldn't fix or replace.

Geno took my arm and asked me, "What do you think baby?". "Well", I said, "it's a great location. You'd be just down from the station to attract the commuters. And there would be people going past, to and from the beach. You could cater to the shoppers, too. You know, it could be a little goldmine. It just needs a little TLC".

"Right", said Geno, "erm, TCP, I think I saw that in the chemist's". "No, Geno", I explained, "TLC". "Oh yes, of course", said Geno, "that's English for 'tender loving care'?". "Well personally", I said, "I was thinking more of 'tantric lusty cuddling', but yeah, let's go with that".

"So", said Geno, "I think I should take the lease on this place". "Now Geno", I said, "let's not get carried away. We need to be practical. We need to have a good look round first. We need to do plenty of prodding and poking". So we had a good look round. There were plenty of power sockets; plumbing for a washing machine and a dishwasher; plenty of storage and space for a fridge and freezer. "Yes", concluded Geno, "I think it will do very nicely". Geno gave a lovely smile; he seemed genuinely happy and excited. The estate agent asked him if he was interested in taking on the tenancy on the place and Geno explained that he was. "Great", said the estate agent, "we can put you on a six month lease to start with and see how you go. If you'd like to come back to the office, we can sort out the paperwork".

As we all walked back to the estate agency, I took Geno's arm and snuggled up to him. "So Geno", I said, "you'll be staying in England for at least the next six months then?" "Oh yes", he said, "I've got a good feeling about this. I really want to put down my roots in your country". "Wonderful, Geno", I said, "you can stick your roots down in my country any time you like".

Back at the estate agency, Geno signed the lease and wrote out a big cheque for the deposit. Well, I shouldn't be surprised; Geno always leaves a big deposit, I don't mind telling you. When he got the keys to the café, Geno seemed so happy. "It's great that you have the keys to your own premises now", I said, "but I hope you know that you already have the keys to my heart". "Thank you, baby", Geno said, and kissed me. "Now, if you have time, perhaps you could help me to clean and sort the place out tomorrow?", Geno asked. "Certainly, love", I replied, "luckily, I don't have to work this weekend, so I'm all yours". It's always a bonus when you get the weekend off work. In fact every week I hope that I can have it off at the weekend, but it doesn't always work out like that.

Sunday 30th August 2015.

We got up early, for a Sunday morning, as we wanted to make the most of the day. Armed with a mop, bucket, brushes, bin bags and numerous sponge scourers, we set out for the café. "Oh Geno", I said, "will you still love me now that you know I'm an old scrubber?" "Of course, Jim", he replied, "now let's enjoy our dirty weekend!"

We got to the café and Geno opened up. I mean he unlocked the door. It was still quite dark, but we couldn't get the lights to come on. "Check the bulbs, Geno", I said; "Here, let me help you. You've got to screw it in tightly". Once we got the lights on, I started sweeping the floors. I cleaned and disinfected the work surfaces and then set about mopping the floors. Geno opened the windows to let in some fresh air, and soon the café was looking fresh and bright. Geno started cleaning the windows; his muscular arms working in a circular motion and making quick work of removing the dirt and grime. "Oh Geno", I said, "you have a wonderful technique there! So strong and manly. You're going to make someone a wonderful husband someday". "Thank you, baby", said Geno; "I hope so".

Later, we turned our attention to the back, and started cleaning the kitchen and store-room. "We'd better take a look at the back yard", I said and Geno fumbled with the keys to open the back door. Honestly, you should have seen the state of Geno's back passage! It was all over-grown with weeds everywhere. "I never thought I would say this", I said, "but I think we need to prune these bushes a bit". "Yes", agreed Geno, "Jim, would you mind popping out to pick up a big chopper for me?" "Oh, it would be my pleasure", I replied, and I set off down South Road to the DIY shop to get a pair of shears. After we had trimmed back the bushes and weeded and swept the back yard, I am pleased to report that Geno's back passage was looking a lot more presentable. Just the way I like it.

In the afternoon, Geno drove the ice cream van over to Ikea, to get a couple of new tables and chairs. It's huge in there, but we found our way round in the end. When we got the flat-packed stuff back to the café, I set about screwing all afternoon to put it all together. It's fair to say that by the time the evening came, we were knackered. But it had been very productive; the café was starting to look very shiny and bright and Geno and I were very tired but very happy and gay.

"Thank you so much for all your help, Jim", Geno said, "Now come on, let's go down to the Queens for a bit of supper. My treat". "Well, that sounds very appropriate", I said. So we locked up the café and walked down the South Road to the Queens. Inside, we had a look at the menus. Geno was having the steak, and I was happy with a tomato pasta. "Are you sure you're OK with that?", Geno asked; "You need to keep your strength up. I can't imagine a life without meat". "Well in fairness, Geno", I replied, "my life is not entirely without meat, is it?"

While we were eating and chatting, a Madonna song came on the jukebox, and Geno became very excited. "Oh, I love Madonna", he said; "I remember she used to sing 'Like a Virgin'". "Yes", I said, "but not for long".

After a great meal, we walked back to Geno's flat, tired but happy. We fed Clara, then, after a quick shower, fell happily into each other's arms. "Oh Geno, baby, I am tired. Please be gentle with me", I said. "OK, baby", he replied. "No, on the other hand Geno, please *don't* be gentle with me!", I quickly corrected myself. "Jim, will you make your flippin' mind up?!", he said.

Monday 31st August 2015.

It's really nice to have an extra day off with the bank holiday. I treated Geno to breakfast in bed. A full English breakfast. You know what a full English breakfast is: twenty ciggies and a pot of tea. No, seriously, I did him a fry up. Well a grill up, to be a bit healthier. Well, whatever it was, it was well-done enough to set the smoke alarm off. Still, it was worth it. It gave me so much pleasure to see Geno contentedly munching away on my black pudding. (Well, it was certainly black by the time he had finished with it!).

"Thank you Jim", he said; "You have been so kind to me. I was wondering if I could trouble you further with a little favour?" "Anything, Geno", I said, "You ask away, love. Help yourself". "Could you help me a bit more in the café today?", he asked. "Certainly", I said, "I'd love to".

Geno explained that he was hoping to get some second-hand appliances just to use in the café for now. For starters, he could do with a fridge, freezer, dishwasher and a washing machine for the towels and tablecloths. He started looking through the free-ads in the paper and made a few calls. When he was ready, we climbed into the ice cream van, and we were off.

The first stop was to pick up the fridge. Geno knocked on the door of the house and we were taken round to the garage to inspect this larder fridge. It seemed in good condition and had plenty of storage space. Geno was about to tip it backwards, so it could be carried horizontally into the ice cream van, when I stopped him. "Oh no, Geno", I said, "you mustn't do that. You're much better off doing it standing up. If you lay it down, the oil from the motor can get mixed in with the gases, so it won't work. You know, you can get into a real mess when you go on your back". "Yes, I know", agreed Geno.

We managed to get the fridge into the ice cream van upright, and we took it round to the café and left it to stand so that the gases could settle. The next stop was to pick up the washing machine. When we got to the house, we checked the washing machine over and I made sure that the drum turned freely. Before we loaded the washer into the ice cream van, I advised Geno that we needed to put the transit bolts in. "We better had, Geno", I said; "you don't want to ruin the suspension on the washer". Mind you, how the pair of us haven't already ruined the suspension on the ice cream van I will never know. The guy who was selling the washing machine passed us the transit bolts, and Geno started stabbing away at the back. (Well, he's good at that, let's be honest). "Here, let me help you, Geno", I said, "Look, you have to get the angle right if you want to penetrate deeply". "Well I've never had any complaints before!", he said. I slid the bolts in all the way and turned them to lock the drum in position. "There you go", I said, "safe and sound. Now there won't be any rolling around until we get back to the café". "I can't wait", Geno said.

You should have seen us struggling to unload the appliances outside the café. It took a bit longer than expected. A traffic warden came along and warned us that we couldn't park there for long. He threatened us with a parking ticket. I really didn't want Geno to get a ticket and so I had to get down on my knees and beg. Not for the first time, admittedly.

When we finally finished getting all the appliances in to the café, I helped Geno push the fridge and freezer into position. Then I set about plumbing in the dishwasher and the washing machine. "Oh Jim", said Geno, "it's very kind of you to sort out my plumbing like that". "Not at all", I said, "it's only fair. After all you have sorted out my plumbing and pipes on many occasions, Geno".

Geno had some lovely linen tablecloths in the red, white and green colours of the Italian flag. He put the white ones into the washing machine first, and started the cycle. It was only later that I realised that he had trapped a corner of one of the tablecloths in the door, and the machine was starting to leak from the door. "Oh Geno!", I scolded, "Just look at you dribbling down your front". I quickly paused the wash, and opened the door to free the tablecloth and rearrange it safely inside the drum. "Oh, thank you Jim", said Geno; "What would I do without you? I do like to have a good man behind me". "Don't we all, mate", I replied. When I restarted the wash cycle, I noticed that there was still a bit of a leak coming from the door. Upon closer inspection, I saw that there was a small rip in the rubber door seal. Honestly, a split rubber! You would think that Geno would be more careful, being a gay man. There's no way round it; we're going to have to get a new rubber. And the thicker the better.

When we had finished cleaning and tidying up the café, I took a moment to survey our handiwork. The café was really starting to sparkle now. I held Geno close and kissed him. "You know, baby", I said, "this place is really starting to look very cosy and homely. Things are really starting to come together. I think the end is in sight". "Is it?", Geno asked, hastily checking his fly.

"Come on, let me treat you to some supper", said Geno, once he had finished adjusting his trousers. "You look famished, Jim", he said; "It looks like you could do with nibbling on a little breadstick". "To be honest, love", I replied, "I could do with nibbling on something rather more substantial than a breadstick". "Certainly", said Geno, "but let's have supper first".

We locked up the café and then happily walked over to the bus stop to catch the bus into town for a bite to eat. We chatted happily on the bus; I was so keen to hear all about Geno's menu ideas and plans for his *gelateria*. It will not be long before the café / *gelateria* opens.

After supper, we had a little stroll, and went to get the bus back to Crosby. Upstairs on the bus, Geno put his arm around me and started singing softly. "What is that you're singing?", I asked. "Oh, it's called *'Dormi, Dormi, Bambin'*", Geno replied; "It's like an Italian lullaby and Christmas carol". "Well, it's beautiful", I said; "And so are you". Geno lifted his head up and had a look around. "Look Jim", he said, "We're the only people on the bus". I replied: "What with your singing, Geno, I'm not surprised".

When we got off the bus, we walked down to Geno's flat. When we went inside, he said, "Jim, you look really tired. You should come and relax. Come and put your legs up". "Thank you, baby", I said, "but in English we usually say 'put your feet up', when you are inviting someone to sit on the sofa". "Jim", Geno went on, "I wasn't thinking about sitting on the sofa". Honestly, that lad has got a one-track mind. Which is very lucky for me. Goodnight.

Tuesday 1st September 2015.

Back to work today, and it was mad busy after the bank holiday weekend. The technical manager wanted me doing technical work and the operations manager wanted me helping the customers on the phone. I felt that I was being pulled in different directions (not in a good way). Honestly, I'm really not used to having all these men fighting over me.

Geno picked me up in the ice cream van after work. He had asked me if I would like to join him on a little trip to the Trafford Centre in the evening. Of course I said yes. I love it when Geno takes me up the Trafford Centre. Well, I like it when he takes me up anywhere, let's be honest.

We had a lovely evening together strolling around the Trafford Centre. Geno was looking for some pictures, vases and general knick-knacks to brighten up the café. One thing I don't understand is why they call the big shop 'Selfridges'. They don't sell fridges at all. They sell all kinds of different stuff.

Still, the café is coming along very nicely. Geno says he hopes to be ready to open by the weekend. I do hope that Geno is open at the weekend; that will really give me something to look forward to.

Wednesday 2nd September 2015.

Mad busy at work again today. You know me, I always like to keep busy and work too many hours. I think I'm getting a bit run down and coming down with a cold. And I've got terrible back ache. I think I've had a chill in my back. Well, I have had worse things in my back over the years, let's face facts. My mate said I should curl up in bed with a Hot Toddy. To be honest, I don't care what his name is, Todd or otherwise, as long as he's hot. No, it looks like I'm destined for an evening in with the Night Nurse. I hope he's cute.

We must be getting into autumn because my asthma is starting to play up. The practice nurse said she would see me after work for my asthma review. "Now Jim", she said, "let's check your technique first of all. I want you to stick this in your mouth and breathe deeply". "Where have I heard that before?", I thought. "Very good, Jim", the nurse continued; "You have a very good technique. Now, I want you to make sure you have two puffs every morning". "Chance would be a fine thing", I thought. And with my clean-ish bill of health, I went home.

Thursday 3rd September 2015.

I felt a lot better today. Yes, I can thoroughly recommend a night in with the Night Nurse and a Hot Toddy. Geno asked if he could meet me after work. He was hoping to have a stroll around the shops at Liverpool One, as he was on the lookout for some napkins and bits and bobs for the café. Knowing me, I'd be more likely to be on the lookout for store detectives.

We met in town after work. I kissed and hugged Geno, and held him close. I felt sure that it must have been a couple of months since I last saw him, even though, of course, it had only been a couple of days. We walked around Liverpool One happily. We got some napkins, in the signature red, white and green colours, and then enjoyed a stroll. Geno was also after a new shirt, and he took me into this trendy American clothes shop. It was really quite dark inside, so much so that it was difficult to make out the colours. I could have sworn that I saw a pit pony pulling the sale rack along. I don't know why there are so many hot guys in these trendy shops. Why are there so many good-looking guys? I mean proper gorgeous. I'm sure they do it on purpose. I mean, no-one needs to be that good-looking. It's just being greedy. Ah well, at least I'm not bitter.

Friday 4th September 2015.

It's nearly the weekend! It's funny how these short weeks with a bank holiday never feel like short weeks. Still, never mind, there's plenty of excitement to look forward to this weekend, as it is the Grand Opening of *Geno's Gelateria* tomorrow. Mind you, in my eyes, Geno has always had a grand opening!

Geno picked me up from work, and we went for a spin in the ice cream van. He needed to pop into B&Q to pick up a few last-minute items, including bins and coat hooks. He said he felt like he had been living in B&Q this week, what with all the preparations for the café. Also on the retail park was a large bedroom store. They were advertising a special offer on mattresses. The poster promised 'bedtime bliss for only £9.99 per month'. £9.99 a month!! Where do I sign up?!

We took the bits back to the café. Outside the café, Geno showed me that he had had the sign-painter out and they had made a lovely sign proudly proclaiming *'Geno's Gelateria'*. There were pictures of Italian flags, and tasteful depictions of landmarks like the Vatican and the Coliseum. And you should have seen the way the painter captured Geno's cones and beautiful balls of ice cream and *gelato*. They really bore a remarkable likeness to Geno's balls.

Once inside the café, Geno positioned the bins, while I set about screwing the coat hooks to the wall. "Isn't this typical?", I thought to myself; "Here I am again, up against a wall, screwing. It's like the story of my life".

Then Geno said we had better be getting off to have an early night as it would be such a busy day tomorrow. "We need to be in early in the morning", Geno said; "Jim, you have helped me so much, and so I really want you to be the first person to sample my wares in the morning". "Thank you baby", I said, "but I've heard that line before. I doubt very much that I am the first guy to sample your wares".

Geno kissed me and said, "Come on, love; let's get to bed. Are you ready for the big opening?" "Oh, I'm always ready for your big opening, Geno!" But then the penny dropped: "Sorry, love", I said, "You're talking about the café, aren't you?"

Chapter 5.

Saturday 5th September 2015

Geno got me up very early this morning. Well, he can get me up any time he likes, to be honest. He was up at the crack of dawn, baking beautiful pastries. Lucky Dawn, that's all I can say. We loaded up the ice cream van with trays of delicious food and went down to the café to open up.

It was lovely seeing the new *'Gino's Gelateria'* sign again, this time in the morning sunlight. It was so bright and colourful. "The sign-writer has done a great job", I said. "Oh yes", agreed Geno, "he's a great guy called Keith; a really talented artist. He's very big in shop-fronts". "Yes, I can see why", I said, "and you, my love, are very big in Y-fronts". Geno laughed. "You know what I mean", he said, "I was talking about shop-fitting". "Ah, not really my thing", I replied, "I'm more into shop-lifting".

Geno unlocked the door to the café and we went inside. We started filling up the display cabinets with all the lovely pastries. Geno started filling the display freezer with all the different flavours of ice cream and *gelato*. "Oh Geno", I teased, "I love it when you dispense your beautiful ice cream. And I never knew it came in so many different flavours!" "Thank you, darling", he said, "but please can we stick to the job in hand?" Blimey, I know what sort of job I'd like to have in hand at the moment. I don't know what's wrong with me; I just can't seem to concentrate. I think it was the sight of Geno bending over the chest freezer that got me going; I got a real eye-full. I don't think I'll ever be able to go into Iceland again. I just need to try and focus and be professional. I think it's going to be quite a trying day for me.

So I tried to focus. I filled the coffee maker and boiler with water and switched them on to pre-heat. I poured the beans into the coffee maker and popped over the road to buy plenty of milk. "The coffee maker is ready to go, I think", I said to Geno, "or do you need me to clean your nozzle?" As soon as I had said that, I wished I hadn't. It caused all sorts of wild images to start swimming around my mind. "It's OK, Jim", Geno said, "my nozzle is as clean as a whistle". "Well, I'm more than happy to wet your whistle if you want", I said. "I clean my nozzle every day with a cocktail stick", Geno explained; "you see I like to have a little prick in my nozzle as it helps to keep the blow-hole clear and then all the steam can come out". I could feel myself about to faint. "Now", continued Geno, "let me show you how to make the perfect cappuccino. You see a good cappuccino is all about thirds. One third espresso coffee, one third hot milk and one third froth". "Hmm", I daydreamed, "hot milk and froth..." "Yes Jim", Geno went on, "it's good to have plenty of creamy froth on top to sip". "Yes indeed", I said, feeling like I was about to explode. Geno took a pre-heated cup and dispensed an espresso coffee into it. Then he poured some milk into a metal jug, to half fill it, and turned on the steam function on the coffee maker. "Now see what I do with my nozzle", Geno said; "First I stick it down into the bottom as far as I can to heat the milk. Then I put the tip of my nozzle just under the surface to froth the top". I could feel my knees starting to buckle. "Oh Geno", I said, "it's so wonderful to watch a skilled master at work", as he handed me his cappuccino, complete with all his hot froth.

"Now Jim", Geno continued, "I want to keep my promise to you". "My goodness", I said, "I've never heard that from a bloke before".

"I'm being serious, Jim", said Geno, "I said I wanted you to be the first to sample my wares, and I really do". "Oh, thank you, Geno", I whispered, leaning in to kiss him. "Please choose a pastry", Geno said. "Oh, they all look so tasty", I said, surveying his wonderful creations. In the end I chose a big pink puff. Not for the first time in my life, I must admit. "They're made with eggs, flour, sugar, and love", he said.

Once we had finished setting up shop, it was nearly 8 a.m. Geno asked me if I would please go over to the train station to hand out leaflets advertising the café. I'm not sure why Geno thought I would be a natural at hanging around outside train stations flogging things. I guess he knows me much better than I realised. It proved to be a smart marketing move, though, as I spoke to many people heading for the train and getting off the train who would be grateful for a hot brew.

Once I had finished handing out the leaflets, I returned to the café and was pleased to see a fair number of punters (sorry, I mean customers) sitting down enjoying hot drinks and pastries for breakfast. As the morning went on, it was lovely to see parents bringing their children in to try the ice creams. Geno's cones were magnificent as always. Later on, Geno asked if I would please serve on the counter while he went to make a start on a pasta carbonara for lunchtime. Of course I said, "No problem". I especially enjoyed serving up the ice creams. I'm now fairly proficient with an ice cream scoop. Well, it's always good to get some extra practise at rolling balls.

At lunchtime, a beautiful young woman came into the café. She started making eyes at Geno. She must have thought I was blind. Well I'm not. She asked me about the lunch menu and explained that she was looking for a hot, spicy Italian dish. "Aren't we all, love?", I said, "Now, do you mind? There's a queue here for hot Italians and I'm at the head of the line!"

As the afternoon went on, a steady stream of shoppers came in for afternoon tea, enjoying cakes and paninis. When it came to closing time, Geno counted up the day's takings. "Pretty good for the first day", Geno said; "If we carry on having this many customers, I'm going to have to get an extension". "Oh no, Geno", I pleaded, "You certainly don't need an extension, love. You're not shagging the Mersey Tunnel, you know".

Sunday 6th September 2015.

Geno got up early this morning as he was going to open up the café to offer a brunch service. "Let me come with you to help, Geno", I said. "Oh Jim", he replied, "I can't ask you to give up your whole weekend to help me". "Geno", I said, "it would be my pleasure. You should know that I am always willing to drop everything for you (especially my pants)".

It was busy at the café. It seems that people were willing to queue up for a nibble on Geno's pastrami. I suppose I shouldn't be surprised. And people were drooling over his hot buns. Everyone was desperate to lick Geno's ices. And don't get me started on his pizzas. People were dying to try his hot pizza, and were asking him to pile on the toppings. Those had better be the only kind of toppings he has been giving people. And of course, everybody loved his hot sweet coffee. It's such a good thing that I'm not a jealous guy.

Geno did brisk business all morning (I thought that was usually my forte); and we closed up at about 1pm. We cleaned and tidied the café, and then stocked up the ice cream van to go down to the beach for the Sunday afternoon crowds. Again, Geno's success seemed to follow him, as we did a brisk trade in soft scoop ices, lollies, drinks and sweets. I must admit, though I'm getting better at pulling down on the ice cream machine lever to do the cones. It's all in the wrist action, you know. I'm glad I can pull that lever, though; it's about the only thing I can pull, let's be honest.

By the time we finally got back to Geno's flat, we were exhausted. We had a little lay down and happily fell asleep for a while in each other's arms. A little while later, I sensed that Geno was stirring. I mean, he was starting to wake up; unfortunately nothing else was stirring at the time. I kissed Geno gently, and said "Baby, you can't carry on working all these hours, seven days a week. You can't keep burning the candle at both ends, even though you know that I really enjoy blowing your candle out". "Yes", said Geno, "I know what you mean. I need some help". "Well, you're a successful businessman", I said, "and if you are going to continue to grow like this, then you will need good people behind you".

Geno thought about this for a moment, and said, 'Jim, I know that we haven't known each other very long, but we seem to get on so well. I was wondering if you might consider coming to work with me full time?". "Oh Geno", I said, "you know I would love that more than anything, and I will always do what I can to help and support you, but I really cannot give up my job at the cooker factory. These cookers won't fix themselves, you know". "I appreciate that", said Geno, "I know that you have your own career that you are committed to". "Well, yes", I said, "sometimes I think that I do need to be committed to some sort of an institution! But one thing's for sure, you do need an assistant, Geno". Geno nodded. "You could certainly use a helping hand, Geno", I said. Geno grinned, and his eyes lit up. "Perhaps

Geno", I continued, "I could come over after work tomorrow and help you to draft an advert so we can get you a little assistant". "I think", Geno replied, "that I would prefer a big assistant", and kissed me. "Well Geno", I said, "it certainly looks like you have an opening which needs filling".

Monday 7th September 2015.

After work, I went round to Geno's flat to help him with his advert for a catering assistant. "Now Geno", I said, "it's important that you list all the qualities that you are looking for". "Yes", agreed Geno, "I was thinking about a cute guy in his twenties, with a tanned, gym-toned body and blue eyes. Those are the sorts of attributes that I'm looking for". "Yes, I bet you are", I hissed, "but I think it would be better to look for someone reliable with catering experience and good customer care skills?" "Yes", I suppose you're right", Geno said, "but I can dream, can't I?"

"Come on, Geno", I said, "Have a go at writing your advert and I'll have a look over it". So Geno wrote a few lines down. "Great", I said when I read them, "but you know, when you say you're 'looking for a guy with a big chopper who's not afraid to get hot and steamy in the kitchen', well, that could be misinterpreted a bit".

I helped Geno rephrase the advert a bit, just to make it a bit clearer that we were looking for a catering assistant and not a 'gentleman of the night'. The advert would be in the paper on Thursday, and on the internet from tomorrow onwards, so we hoped to get some response soon. "Here you go, Geno", I said, "let me help you get that advert over to the paper and on the website. I'll just whip out my Samsung Galaxy Note smart-phone". "Well", said Geno, "you're very welcome to whip out anything you like. But, that phone's big enough, isn't it?!". "Yes mate", I replied, "I always like to have a big phone. I think I'm compensating for something". "What's that?", Geno asked. "My eyesight", I replied.

Tuesday 8th September 2015.

I said I would pop round to Geno's after work to help him sift through any e-mail responses he had had to the job advert. I popped in and said, "Hi Geno, how is your mailbox doing?". "A bit sore, to be honest", he replied, "but missing you desperately". "Oh, I'm sorry to hear that, angel", I said, "but I meant your e-mail inbox, not your 'male box'". "Oh, I see", said Geno, "Right, let's have a look at the computer". I gently shooed Clara off the computer and turned it on. "Honestly, Geno", I said, "just because it's called a 'lap-top' doesn't mean that you should let Clara sleep on top of it".

When the computer had booted up, I opened up the e-mails. "Wow, Geno", I said, "it looks like you've had a good response. Look at all these e-mails!" I had a good flick through (the e-mails) and it looked like there had been at least 15 come in. I looked through the e-mail addresses and said, "You know, it looks like a lot of people are using hotmail.co.uk nowadays. Oh well, Geno, I don't need Hotmail 'cos I'm so lucky to have you as my Hot Male". "Thank you, Jim", said Geno, as he kissed me.

We sifted through the e-mails together. "What about this guy called Scott?", Geno asked; "He says in his CV that he is very good with his hands!". "Yes, Geno", I said, "but I know you too well. His CV also says that he took his GCSEs in 2009, so I don't think he could be more than 22!! And so you're old enough to be his father. Honestly, Geno, people would think you got him from ToyBoys R Us!".

"How about this lady?", I said, looking through some more of the e-mails. "She's done 3 years in a posh bistro doing food prep", I said, reading her CV. "She's called 'Lucy'", I continued, "and she says she's a dab hand with an industrial dishwasher and she's very experienced with bleach, by all accounts". "I don't care if she bleaches her hair!", Geno exclaimed; "Jim, I think you just want me to hire a woman so that I won't be tempted! Honestly, you're so jealous sometimes!" "Oh Geno", I said, "I'm sorry; you are so special to me, Geno; I don't mean to be jealous. But I must admit, it would be a novelty for you to have a woman working under you. I never thought I would see the day when you would hire a woman!" "Very funny", said Geno. "Well Geno", I said, "It's important to look at who is best for the job. Sure you need to fill the counter with delicious treats and candies, but you don't need eye candy behind the counter as well".

I helped Geno to work through the applications to identify those with relevant experience to invite for interview, and to see which ones needed to be politely declined. When we had finished, we had 4 who definitely needed to go on the short list. We needed to wait for the main response from the paper on Thursday before finalising arrangements. As were finishing up, Geno said, "Oh look Jim, here's one more e-mail. This guy is called Hank, and he's included a photo in with his application. He looks really ripped and toned!" I took a look. "Oh, no, Geno, love", I said, "I don't think it is a response to the job advert. It looks more like an e-mail to do with your subscription to *Hot Muscle Weekly*".

Wednesday 9th September 2015.

Geno's job advert will be in the paper tomorrow, so I advised Geno to brace himself for an influx of calls. I explained that it would be a good idea to jot down a few questions to ask the applicants to help identify who would be suitable for interview. "Come on, Geno", I said, "Let's get some questions together. It will be fun". "But I'm not very good at asking and answering questions", he replied. "Of course you are", I said, "I mean you're always helping the police with their enquiries, aren't you?"

After a bit of brain-storming, Geno sat down to write out some questions. After a while, I said, "How are you getting on Geno? Come on, let's have a look". As I glanced down the list of questions, I must say I was a bit concerned. "Geno", I said, "I'm not entirely sure that these questions are appropriate or professional". "What do you mean?", he asked. "Well", I explained, as gently as I could, "here you are asking what the applicant's ideal first date would be, and here you are asking the applicant if they are attracted to boys, girls or boys and girls. You know, I think a lot of people would be offended by these questions, and they might very well give the impression that you wanted to hook up with them. Tell me honestly, Geno, are you quite sure I am sufficient to fulfil your romantic desires? It seems to me that you want to surround yourself with attractive young men in the café!" "Oh Jim", he said, "you know that I love you. You know that I only have eyes for you. I just think that it is important that I know a bit about the person who is working under me". "Well yes", I said, "it's certainly nice to take an interest in your employees, but surely you don't need to probe them so deeply and intimately!" "Well, that's half the fun!", Geno replied.

Right, well this conversation was getting way too bizarre, and I really had to rein Geno in (not for the first time, I might add). Geno could get into serious trouble with these questions, so I wrote out some more suitable suggestions. Before long, we had a quick checklist to ascertain the applicant's relevant work experience, availability to start work, and motivation as to why they wanted to work at the café. Sometimes Geno just needs a little help in focussing on the bigger picture. (He doesn't need any help in focussing on young men). I'm too good to that lad, I really am.

"Now Geno", I said, "let's get some sleep. I think you are going to get a lot of phone calls tomorrow". I kissed him and fell into his arms, as we happily drifted off to sleep.

Thursday 10th September 2015.

I ran over to Geno's café after work as quickly as I could to help with the response to the job advert. I honestly haven't answered so many phone calls in a long time, not since that time I did a stint as an operator on a premium rate, erm, telephone helpline. I still remember the advert jingle: "If you're lonely and have no fun at home, then chat and flirt on the telephone!" Oh yes, it was a very classy service that we were providing. My job was to chat to each caller to see what sort of person they were looking for and then put them through to a like-minded soulmate they could chat to and flirt with. I suppose I was like a cross between Cilla Black and the speaking clock. I loved match-making. Sadly, my career came to a premature end one fateful Thursday night when I accidentally hooked up a vicar who had misdialled with a pole dancer (and I don't mean a dancer from Poland). You should have seen the headlines: 'Randy Rev Stalks Sultry Stripper'. I was proper mortified. And the vicar was defrocked. In more ways than one. Still, at least I had learnt a lot of useful skills of empathy and concern. Perhaps I should volunteer for the Sanatogens.

Sorry, I digress. I answered the phone in the café, and my first call was from a lovely lady called Marion. Or so I thought. When I questioned her, she said that she didn't have a lot of catering experience as such, but she had once threatened her husband with a meat cleaver and wondered whether that would count? Well, I thanked her for her interest but politely explained that we needed more experience. So she said she would phone back once she had managed to actually chop her husband up with the meat cleaver. I explained that we did not want people to be causing grievous bodily harm, but we did want people who could prepare delicious food. "After all", I said, "the way to a man's heart is through his stomach". "No", she corrected me, "the way to a man's heart is straight through the swine's chest with a pickaxe". You know, I think she might have some unresolved anger issues.

My next call came from a lovely guy called Tim. He had worked extensively in treacle and had also gained experience in squeezing lemons. "Wow", I thought, "sticky, sweet and sour; what a versatile guy!" He seemed very suitable, so I invited him to come in for interview. My only concern was that Geno might well get the wrong end of the stick if Tim asks him if he can squeeze his lemons.

After a few more calls, I spoke to a great lady called Veronica. She had just returned from a very successful summer pressing grapes in Spain. Prior to this, she had been involved in scooping ice cream and could even spin sugar into candyfloss using either hand. Wow, an ambidextrous twirler! She sounded like a natural, so of course I invited her in for interview.

All in all, I managed to get 4 definitely good applicants for interview, which meant we had 8 in total, including the e-mail applications. Geno arranged for these 8 to come in to the café for interview tomorrow afternoon at closing time. It was going to be a fairly informal type of interview. We were going to do some practical catering tests and then have a chat about hours of work, wages and practical stuff. I said I would try to get back from the factory as early as possible to help with the interviews.

Geno thanked me for all my help. I kissed him and held him tightly, and said "You're welcome, baby". "I'm so excited", Geno said, "Just think, soon I will hopefully have someone to give me a helping hand around the place". I shot Geno a little wink. "Well Geno", I said , "knowing the size of your bits, you could certainly do with someone to give you a helping hand! And perhaps you already have a certain someone to help you?! Let's lock up the café and go home". Geno kissed me, and we happily set about cleaning and tidying the café, ready to lock up. When we had finished, we walked back to Geno's flat, lovingly holding hands and kissing all the way. I feel that it is only appropriate to quote the Vernons Girls at this point: 'I went funny all over' and 'Boy did I know that I'd been kissed'! And of course later, when we were in the shower, 'When the room is steamy, oh, he looks so dreamy; curly hair and six feet tall'! I'm sorry, I'm showing my age again.

Friday 11th September 2015.

So I went over to the café as quickly as I could after work. When I arrived, I saw that poor Geno was in a bit of a state. "What's the matter, love?", I asked. "Oh Jim, I'm in a panic", Geno said; "The applicants are due to arrive in half an hour, and I think I can hear terrible scratching in the kitchen. I think that perhaps a mouse has got in through my back passage". "Ow", I said, "that sounds really uncomfortable. I think we had better take a look".

Out in the back kitchen, I had a good look round. I could definitely hear some scratching coming from underneath the cupboards. "Environmental Health would have a field-day over this", I said; "We are going to have to try to get it out. Geno, tell me, do you know if this kick-plate plinth under the cupboards comes off?" "Well, to be honest, Jim", Geno said, "I've never had it off, and I think it may be sealed up". I tried to keep a straight face. I really did. "Geno", I said, "I find that very hard to believe".

After some gentle pulling on the kick-plate plinth, I did manage to have it off. Fortunately, it was just one little mouse under the cupboards. Nothing bigger or scarier. We managed to get it into a box so we could let it go free outside. "Right", I said, "panic over. Let's get ready to greet the applicants".

At 5 p.m., the eight applicants arrived, and we welcomed them in to the café. Geno gave a brief lesson in how to operate the coffee machine and showed everyone the best way to handle his nozzle. Then we put them through their paces serving up coffees and warming pastries. Geno and I had to sit at one of the tables and pretend to be customers! Well, it wasn't the first time we had indulged in a little bit of role play, let's be honest. Geno pretended to be an awkward customer and was complaining that his coffee was cold. I was really proud of the way the applicants politely handled him. It was no mean feat. After all, I have had a lot of experience of handling Geno, and I still find it quite challenging. After the practical activities, we then had a chat with each of the applicants in turn.

Once all of the assessments and interviews had been completed, we sat all the applicants down with coffee and cakes, while Geno and I withdrew to the back kitchen to compare notes. To be honest, it came as no surprise that Lucy stood out as the best candidate. The things she could do with marshmallows and whipped cream were just out of this world. She really was head and shoulders above the rest. (I don't mean to say that she had dandruff. Her hair was lovely). We had discovered when chatting to Lucy that she liked to be called 'Luce' for short (pronounced 'Loose'). I joked with Geno that he would soon have a loose woman working under him, and indeed he thought it was very appropriate. So, we spoke to the applicants one by one to congratulate Lucy and to thank and commiserate with the others. Lucy was available to start the next day and she was very keen to get cracking and get her hands on Geno's utensils. She wasn't the only one. We thanked everyone for coming and then we set about tidying and locking up the café.

As we walked back to Geno's flat, I felt happy and relaxed. It was a weight off my mind to know that Geno wouldn't have to handle all the work by himself. He now had a good woman behind him. (He already had a good man behind him, believe me). "Jim", he said, "I just want to thank you for all your help in the café and with the recruitment. I know you are busy with your own job, and I'm so grateful that you give your time to me". "Oh Geno", I said, "don't be daft. You know that I would do anything to help you. It is a labour of love". He kissed me gently. "Please let me take you out tomorrow night", Geno said; "My treat. I want to say thank you properly". "That would be great, Geno", I said; "I can't wait to be seen around town with a handsome Italian on my arm. And if he's not available, Geno, perhaps you could stand in instead?" Geno laughed. "Well Jim", he said, "It will give us a chance to relax, dance and catch up. Hopefully a chance to chat too. There's something that I've been meaning to ask you".

Chapter 6.

Saturday 12th September 2015.

Geno's taking me out tonight! He wants to take me for a little drink and a dance to thank me for my help at the café. I'd better go and make myself look beautiful. No there isn't enough time for that. I'd better just try to make myself look presentable. Hmm, that might still take quite a while. I'd better get cracking. Now where did I put my slap? I can't find my lip-gloss anywhere. And it was my favourite shade – 'brazen berry'. I love that shade; it captures my personality perfectly.

....

I had arranged to meet Geno in a gay pub in town at 8 p.m. I got to the pub a little early, and ordered a drink. The bingo was in full swing. A chap started chatting to me: "Are you playing bingo?", he asked. "No mate, I'm just waiting for my friend", I replied, not quite sure how to describe my relationship with Geno. "Oh right", he said, "I'm just waiting to meet my wife". "Wow", I said, "your wife must be very understanding. Doesn't she mind meeting you in a gay pub?" "Oh no", he replied, "she's just been shopping. I'm not gay, but I like to come to gay bars because I like getting attention from guys". "Oh I see", I said, a bit confused, I must admit, "well you're very welcome; it's good to have you on board". I wonder if this situation was like one of those interest-free credit offers in the big furniture showrooms, you know 'bi now, gay later'.

The chap went on: "I really like gay guys. You have got the guts to stand up and say who you are, and what you want". "Thank you", I said. "And what do I want from life?", I thought to myself; "I never thought I would feel like this. I never thought this would happen. But I want to be with Geno. Forever".

Just then Geno arrived. He came over and hugged me. The guy I had been chatting to said, "You two look like you'd make a great couple". "Thank you", I said, "Geno's a great guy". "You look like a natural couple; you look like you've known each other for ages", the chap said. "Well, not really", I said, "just a month or so". "Well, I think you'd be good together", he said, "Why don't you give him a kiss?". He then nicked my glasses off my face and said he wouldn't give them back until I kissed Geno. Well, I didn't need to be asked twice. I took Geno in my arms and kissed him deeply and passionately. I suppose it's a good thing that chap had removed my specs 'cos they would have definitely steamed up. I needed to get my specs back, though, because they were quite expensive. That's the problem with clarivocals. And besides, Geno seems to like them; he's always saying that I have great specs appeal. I managed to get my specs back, but I couldn't stop kissing Geno. And as the evening went on, we couldn't stop dancing either, or hugging come to think of it.

Geno went to the bar and ordered champagne cocktails. "Blimey Geno", I said, "you're pushing the boat out aren't you?" "What does that mean?", he asked. "Oh, it's just an expression, love", I explained; "It means spending more money than usual or maybe having a bit of luxury". "Oh right", said Geno, "and are you pushing your boat out too, Jim?" "No, love", I replied, "my boat sank a while ago".

As we went round a couple of pubs and clubs, I was amazed at how many people said that Geno and I looked like a great couple. A great couple of what I'm not sure, but many people said we looked happy together and that we should be together. I began to think that they had a point. I was really falling in love with Geno, and I could really imagine being with him for the long term. I could imagine the two of us growing old together. OK, growing older together. Honestly, we're not that old.

I never thought that I would find a man who I could love and who would love me for the long haul. I haven't been very lucky in love. I mean I've been on a few dates with nice guys, but it never led on to anything more. People would always try to encourage me and say, "Don't worry, there's plenty more fish in the sea". Yeah, plenty of fish, but why did I keep catching the crabs?

But Geno is different. I've not known him very long but we have already been through so much together. I had been praying to God for an angel, and it looks like He has sent me one (with a little bit of a horny devil thrown in for good measure). I guess you should be careful what you wish for. I hope we get the chance to have a proper chat soon about our future.

We had a wonderful evening dancing, singing and laughing. At the end of the night, we took a taxi back to Geno's flat in Blundellsands. He really was spoiling me. I was shattered, and really struggled climbing the stairs up to Geno's flat. "Blimey, Geno", I said, "I thought the song said there were only three steps to heaven. You seem to have at least fifty!" "Oh well", Geno replied, "sometimes you have to suffer a little purgatory on the way to heaven, my love".

We made it up to Geno's flat at last and kissed passionately as we held each other tightly in each other's arms. We happily settled down in bed, so happy and content to be in each other's loving arms.

Sunday 13th September 2015.

I was still exhausted when I woke up this morning. Geno had been very wild with me during the night. Very wild. It was like: In. Out. Shake it all about. I thought we were doing the hokey cokey. And, you know, he's gone and bought this air bed. It's very comfy and very bouncy. "You bounce away", I had said to Geno when we first tried it out; "just think of me as your personal trampoline". I must admit, I was terrified of it deflating, but I had the foresight to get a little cycle puncture repair kit from the newsagents the other day. When he had first unpacked the air bed, I must admit I had been very excited because I had thought it was a bouncy castle. I had offered to get my foot pump out to blow it up (I'm very good at pumping and blowing), but apparently my services weren't required because it comes with an electric pump. Very posh. You just push a button and you get a perfect erection in seconds every time. I could certainly do with one of those. What will they think of next? My other concern about the airbed was to do with the weather. "If it keeps raining we'll get flooded out", I had said to Geno, "Then we'll float out of the window and we'll get washed up in New Brighton by morning". I suppose I was being a bit dramatic. It would have to rain an awful lot to flood Geno's flat. He is on the third floor after all.

I'm sorry, I am digressing again. Geno and I lay happily together on the airbed, gazing lovingly into each other's eyes. I hoped this might be a good opportunity to have a chat about our future. "Geno", I said, "you know that I really like you. I'm falling in love with you, although I am trying to take things slowly. Do you think we could have a future together?" "Yes, I do", replied Geno, "I think we make a great team. I think we could be very good together", and he kissed me. "That's lovely Geno", I said, "although I was rather hoping that we might be very bad together!" "Yes, that sounds like a good idea",

Geno replied. "I think it would be helpful if we had a think about our future", I explained. "Yes indeed", Geno said, "we should put our heads together". "That sounds like fun", I grinned.

Geno kissed me again. "Jim", he said, "I love you. You are so good for me. You really make me feel Alice". I was a bit confused. "Who, pray tell, is Alice?", I asked, "and why do you feel the need to feel her?" "Oh, no, sorry love, I have got that wrong", Geno explained; "What is the English? I mean you make me feel alive, that's it". "Thank you, darling", I said; "And you, Geno, you drive me wild. You make me feel so hot and excited all the time!" "That sounds like a very good thing", Geno winked. "Well not really, love", I replied, "I mean I've already been banned from Tesco's 'cos they thought I was nicking cucumbers and stuffing them down my pants".

"Jim, I really want to be with you forever", Geno said. "Thank you angel", I replied, and kissed him tenderly. "Seriously, Jim", Geno went on, "have you thought about having a relationship with a man?" "Yes love, I have", I replied; "Well, to be honest, I've thought about very little else". "I see", said Geno; "And tell me, Jim, do you believe in same-sex marriage?" "Well, no, not really, hun", I said. "No?", asked Geno, sounding rather surprised. "Well, no", I explained; "I think if you had the same sex all the time then you would get rather bored".

"Jim, I want to be honest with you", Geno went on; "I have had relationships before in Italy". "Thank you, my love", I said; "Yes, it's always best to be honest. It's good to be upfront. Mind you, it's good to be up the back as well, come to think of it. I've not had much luck with men. Just a few dates, really". "Ah, tell me about them", Geno asked.

So I told Geno all about my dates. "This shouldn't take too long", I thought. "Well", I began, "all of the guys I have dated have been really lovely. It was always a shame though when I was really fond of a guy but it didn't develop into mutual love, you know what I mean?" "Yes, I understand", Geno said; "It's awful when that happens. It leaves a very bitter taste in the mouth". "Yes", I agreed, "literally".

"The first guy I went out with was very sweet", I explained; "A really nice guy. It's a shame, really; we could have been happily married and living in a maisonette in Tranmere by now". "Well, some things just aren't meant to be", said Geno, sympathising. "There was another lovely guy I met", I continued; "He said that I was a really handsome guy! And, you know, he had a lovely dog and a white stick too". "Very funny", said Geno. "Well, let's be honest", I went on, "that's the beauty of blind dates. If they're blind, they can't see how repulsive I look!" "You're not repulsive, Jim", Geno said; "You're lovely, and I love you". "Thank you, baby", I said, and kissed him again.

"So, are those all of your dates?", Geno asked. "Pretty much", I said; "There was this one guy I dated who was a great pianist. He was very good at playing the organ". "I bet he was!", Geno exclaimed. "Then there was this other guy, but things just didn't feel right, you know? I felt very uncomfortable. No matter how much lubricant he used. I suppose I was just too soft with him. And he was far too hard with me".

"You're really sweet, Jim", Geno said; "It's interesting the way that you describe all your dates as 'lovely'. It's like you always see the best in people". "Well yes", I said, "I think you will find some goodness in everyone, if you look hard enough". "True", said Geno, "but sometimes to find the goodness you have to probe quite deeply". "Now you're talking, mate", I replied.

"Geno, you're such a great guy", I said; "You're so handsome and sweet. What could you possibly see in me? What could I possibly offer a man like you?". "Yourself", Geno replied, "and your love". I kissed him and held him tight. "But I'm nothing special, Geno", I said; "I'm just ordinary. I'm just a guy". "I'm just a guy too", replied Geno. "Well, yes, Geno, I noticed that you were a guy", I said; "There were one or two things that gave it away".

"You're such a sensitive guy, Jim", Geno said. "Do you think so?", I replied. "Well, yes", Geno explained; "I mean you're always writing in your diary, aren't you?" "Well, Geno, you know, it can be a good thing to express your thoughts and feelings", I said. "Well maybe one day they will make a film based on your diary", Geno said. "Blimey, Geno", I said, "I wonder what they'd call it? Maybe 'Fifty Shades of Gay'!"

"Jim, I really love you", Geno said; "I feel like God has given me a precious gift". "Thank you baby", I said, "but you know what they say about gifts". "What's that?", asked Geno. "Well, with gifts", I went on, "you don't always get what you want. But don't worry, I've kept the receipt; you're welcome to take me back to M&S and swap me if you want". "Oh Jim", said Geno, "you are the perfect gift for me. Just what I wanted!" "Well, mate", I said, "if I'm the perfect present, I can't wait until you unwrap me!"

"Jim, I've been meaning to ask you something", said Geno. My heart started to pound as I thought that Geno was about to pop the question. Well, I was hoping that he was going to pop something else, to be honest. Seriously, though, I was terrified in case he was going to make a proposal. Mind you, it can be fun getting propositioned, I suppose. "Yes, Geno", I said, "what would you like to ask?" "Well", he went on, "I've noticed that we are spending a lot of time together in my flat. In fact you don't manage to get home very often". "No, it's true", I said; "My poor sisters think that I've eloped to Gretna Green. Mind you, it has been difficult to get home with all the rain. The road gets flooded all the time. Still, you know me; always organised. I never go anywhere without my rubbers". "Very wise, Jim", said Geno, "but I was thinking that it might be better if you moved in with me. You know it would be great if we could spend more time together and snuggle up together more. Do you think it's a good idea?" "I do", I replied, as I kissed him tenderly.

Monday 14th September 2015.

I went over to Geno's café after work. Geno had been complaining to me about poor suction. "Honestly, Geno", I said, "I've never had any complaints before". "No, not you love", Geno explained. "It's this thing", he said, pointing to the extractor fan; "Would you mind having a look under my hood?" "Certainly, Geno", I said; "It would be my pleasure".

Upon closer inspection, I noticed that the grease filters on the extractor fan were clogged with grease, so I took them down and gave them a good scrub. Looking into the extractor, I saw quite a build-up of grease, dust and fluff. "There's only one thing for it, Geno", I said; "I'm going to have to go right up your flue and clear out all the blockages".

After a good clean out, Geno's flue looked a lot better, and the extractor seemed to work a lot more efficiently. I was so proud to be able to give Geno better suction. Geno kissed me. "Oh Jim", he said, "you are so good to me. We are partners in the finest sense of the word. You help me in the café and you help me at home. I am so grateful to you. And I know you are busy with your own work. Have you had a good day at work? Did you have a good shaft?" I thought about this for a while. "I think, Geno, you may mean 'did I have a good shift'? But yes, it was a good day, thank you". "Let's just tidy up the café", Geno said, "and then let's take the ice cream van over to your house so that you can pick up some stuff". "Great", I said, "I could certainly do with picking up some clothes and stuff".

We got into the ice cream van, and headed out to the countryside to my sisters' house. "It's lovely to see you happy, Jim", my sister said; "Tell me, what is the lucky guy called?" "Well", I said, "the lucky guy is called Jim, but here is the unlucky guy, called Geno!" My sisters hadn't really had the chance to meet Geno properly, so I was pleased to introduce him. Geno was charming, of course and we appeared as a very happy couple. I assured my sisters that I would still do all I could to support them and help them. I packed up my stuff and we said farewell for now as we headed back to Blundellsands.

Geno parked up the ice cream van outside and then we climbed the stairs up to his flat. "Oh, this is so exciting, Geno", I said; "So romantic. Are you going to carry me over the threshold?". "I thought people only did that when they got married", Geno said. "Well, we are practically married", I replied; "After all, I've had your ring on my finger many times, let's be honest".

As I entered Geno's little flat, I was so happy. I kissed him and hugged him. It was wonderful to be together as a couple now. We made some supper together and cuddled together on the sofa. "Oh Geno", I said, "it's so lovely to be with you like this. You know, you have taught me so much, Geno. Love isn't just about exciting nights out or holidays. It's about sharing life together in ordinary, everyday ways, like cuddling up like this". "I see, Jim", said Geno, "so you just want me as a teddy bear to cuddle up with?". 'Well, love, put it this way", I replied; "If you do come down to the woods today, then you're certainly sure of a big surprise!"

I couldn't have been happier, sitting there snuggling up with my dark-haired lover, my very own foot-long Italian. I kissed him and held him tight, hoping that the moment would never end.

Tuesday 15th September 2015.

Well, unfortunately the alarm clock rang, ending the moment. Geno and I got up to get ready for another day's work. "I hope the alarm wasn't too early for you, love", Geno said. "Oh, no, baby", I replied, "I'm quite used to you getting me up early". "Let's grab a shower", Geno suggested. "Thank you, Geno", I said; "Are you sure you don't mind me using your shower?". "Of course not, Jim", Geno replied; "This is your home now. Please help yourself to anything you fancy". "Oh, thank you, Geno", I said; "I certainly will", and I kissed him.

The sight of Geno in the shower was quite an inspiration. The warm water glistened all over his jet black hair and smooth olive-toned skin. His muscles were magnificent. Well, not just his muscles, to be honest. He looked like a work of art; a thing of beauty. He looked like something that had been sculpted by Mike and Angelo. Well, I wouldn't mind chipping away at him, put it that way. Where did I put my chisel? "Oh Geno", I said; "You're so beautiful. You look so fit and healthy, so athletic". "Thank you, love", Geno replied; "We Italians try to keep healthy, with plenty of olive oil". "Oh I see", I said; "Well,

I'm glad you keep yourself well-oiled. That will certainly make things much easier".

When we managed to tear ourselves away from the shower, Geno fixed us a little bit of breakfast. I was so impressed by the way that Geno could unscrew the cap off a bottle of milk with his mouth. "Blimey, mate", I said; "Very impressive! I can tell you've done that before!" After a quick coffee we got dressed and said our goodbyes to get off to work.

It was another busy day at the cooker factory. The boss had asked if I would please give some microwave training to the colleagues. Of course, I said 'yes' and jumped at the chance! I love training as I like to help people learn and it's always such fun!

So we gathered in the training room and I began my presentation. "Now", I said, "firstly let's get an understanding of how microwaves work. Tell me, what substance can be found in all foods and drinks?" I received a variety of interesting answers, including 'salt' and 'additives', but I finally got the answer I was looking for: 'water'. "That's right", I said, "every food and drink contains molecules of water. Microwaves contain a special device called a magnetron, which creates high-powered microwave energy. The microwave energy makes the water molecules jiggle and vibrate so that they knock against each other". (I think that Geno may have a similar contraption because I sometimes hear strange vibrating noises coming out of his flat).

"Now then", I continued, "what happens when two things are rubbed together vigorously?" "Erm, your Geno gets awfully excited?", one of my mates ventured. "Well, that's true", I said, "but I was thinking more about cooking. Try this experiment: rub the palms of your hands together quickly. What do you notice?" I got lots of answers to do with chaffing and heating. "That's right", I said; "The friction produces heat". (Tell me about it). "As the water molecules rub against each other, heat is produced and this heat transfers throughout the food to cook it. So, you see, microwaves do not create an external heat source in the way that a traditional oven does. Instead, the heat is generated in the food itself so that it sort of cooks from the inside out".

"Next, let's look at how we can ensure that food is thoroughly cooked through", I continued; "What can we do to ensure that?" I received some good answers to do with stirring the food half-way through and allowing food to stand at the end to let the heat transfer throughout. "Now", I explained, "microwaves typically use one or two methods to ensure that the microwave energy hits the food evenly. They are: using a turntable to constantly turn the food so that all sides of the food are exposed to the stream of microwave energy, and also sometimes using a wave stirrer to stir the microwave energy so that it hits all parts of the cooking cavity. Believe me, it's really important to feel the energy in all parts of your cavity if you want to experience a satisfactory result. Now, a common concern from consumers is that the turntable will not turn. Why do you think this happens?" As I went round the group, I got some good answers to do with making sure that the turntable function had not been deactivated, that the turntable plate was level, not overloaded and properly inserted into position. "That's right", I said, "proper insertion is indeed the key. But did you know that a common reason for the turntable not to turn is because the user has a dirty ring? You see, if the roller ring is dirty, it cannot roll around easily and this makes it difficult for the turntable to spin properly". To make sure everyone got the point, I demonstrated how to strip down your microwave and give your ring a thorough clean.

"Now we must talk about safety", I said; "You know a lot of people use their microwave to reheat a cup of coffee or tea which has gone cold. But when you heat a liquid like that and then take the cup out of the microwave, you can find that things get to the boil very quickly and overflow creating lots of hot bubbles". "Are you talking about your Geno again?", my mate asked. I ignored this remark and continued, trying to be dignified. "We need to try to avoid this risk of scalding", I said, "Any ideas what we can do?" "Don't fill the cup right to the brim?", suggested one colleague. "That's a really good idea", I said, "and also nowadays kitchen shops sell really good plastic boiling rods which help the liquids to heat evenly and help prevent bubbles forming. So if you can get into the habit of sticking your rod in before you turn up the power, then you should avoid problems".

"Now finally, let's have a look at the types of cookware that work best in microwaves", I said; "Tell me, what material should you avoid using in a microwave?" Everyone agreed on metal. "That's right", I explained; "Microwave energy cannot pass through metal, instead metal reflects the microwaves away. So if you put a metal dish inside the microwave you can get sparks and arcing. It reminds me of that time Geno got his stubble caught on my polyester sheets. You should have seen the sparks fly! The room lit up like Blackpool illuminations! Now what sort of cookware would work better than metal?" We discussed a few options and settled on glass. "Yes, indeed", I said, "heat- resistant glass is a good option because the microwaves can penetrate the glass. Believe me, it's very important to get the right material so that you get effective penetration".

As I came to the end of the training session, I asked if anyone had any questions. Lots of hands shot up. "How long have you been going out with Geno?", "Where did you meet Geno?", "What does Geno do?", "Have you got a photo of Geno?"... They just kept on coming.

Which is just like Geno, come to think of it. I was overwhelmed by everyone's support. But I thought it would be more professional to stick to questions about cooking. Finally, one of my colleagues asked, "So are microwaves safe to use?" "Yes indeed", I said; "It's important that any appliance is used with common sense and according to the instructions. With microwaves it is very important that the door is closing correctly and that there is no damage to the door or seals, to avoid the risk of microwave energy leaking out". "Right", said my colleague, "so was that a 'yes' or a 'no', Jim? Why can't you give a straight answer?" "Sorry", I said, "but sometimes it can be difficult to get a straight answer out of a gay man".

After work, I went over to the flat to meet Geno. I kissed him softly and asked him about his day in the café and selling ice creams. I told him about my day too. "Wow Jim", he said, "you really seem to enjoy your work. Have you worked with cookers for long?" "Oh yes", I said, "for many years now. I'll never forget the first time I fell in love with a range cooker. I was on my knees at the time, inside John Lewis. I just opened the door and the way the grill pan slid out was just poetry in motion!" "I see", said Geno, "but Jim, perhaps you are working too hard. You should try to come out a bit more". "I'm not coming out again, mate", I said; "I haven't recovered after last time. You really shouldn't have to explain your sexuality". "No", Geno continued, "I mean having a good work-life balance". "I do have a good work-life balance", I protested; "Chaos at work, chaos at home; just the way I like it".

"Well, let's eat", said Geno; "Would you like soup and a roll?" "Yes, I'd love to have a roll with you, Geno", I said. It was lovely soup and I really enjoyed sitting on the sofa munching on Geno's buns. As we sat there, Lady Lager came on the radio. "What's that she's singing?", I asked; "'You and me could write a bad romance'? That sounds very appropriate. You know Geno, I'm going to write a book one of these days. Maybe people would be interested to read the diary of a scouse queen". "Yes", agreed Geno, "you should do that. It could be a very interesting read".

"Jim, I really love you", said Geno; "Like I said, we are partners in the finest sense of the word. You have been helping me with the café and helping me with the flat. I can't imagine life without you now. I think it would be good if we became travel partners too". "Well yes, Geno", I said; "You know that I would go to the ends of the earth for you. Well, certainly as far as Southport anyway". "Thank you, darling", Geno said, "but I was thinking of a trip a bit further afield than that. What do you say?"

Chapter 7.

Saturday 3rd October 2015.

So, it's been a good couple of weeks now since I moved in with Geno. It's been wonderful. He completes me and supports me in so many ways. And of course I care for him and look after him. He especially seems to need a lot of help with his laundry. For example, I really had to explain to Geno that just because I said I thought that black underwear was sexy, that didn't mean he should wait a fortnight before washing his vest.

Then there's the ironing, cleaning, tidying and washing up. Yes, it really can be a full-time job being Geno's boyfriend. I make sure that I take plenty of vitamins and supplements. And Geno is very good at helping me to drink plenty of protein.

Yes, it can be a lot of work living together. But of course there are some wonderful benefits. I just love laying next to Geno watching him sleep. He is so beautiful. I feel like Patrick Moore sometimes, spending all night gazing at heavenly bodies. Well, it's fair to say I have developed a keen interest in astronomy since meeting Geno. Or is that anatomy? Well, either way, with the size of Geno's bits you really don't need to use a telescope, believe me.

Just as I was musing away like this, Geno came up and kissed me. "Oh Jim", he said, "I love having you here. Are you happy living with me? Do I make you happy?". "Yes of course you do, love", I replied; "I was so happy and excited when you entered my life. Well, I was hoping you might enter one or two other things, to be honest". "Yes indeed", agreed Geno, "it is wonderful when we consommé our relationship". "Geno, love", I explained; "I think that consommé is a type of soup, you know. That could make things very messy in the bedroom".

"Seriously though Jim", said Geno, "I want you to be happy and fulfilled". "Oh I am love", I said; "Don't you worry. You can fill me full any time you like. Please just help yourself". "I'm trying to be serious, Jim", protested Geno. "So am I, love", I replied; "I love you, Geno. You complete me. You complement my life. You help me to be a better man. When we are apart I feel that half of me is missing. I want to be with you for ever". We kissed and held each other tight. "Oh Jim", said Geno; "That's exactly how I feel. I love you so much. Jim, you won't hurt me or leave me, will you?" "Of course not", I replied; "You know it would be a very foolish man who would turn his back on his lover. Well, unless he was preparing for a particular type of intimacy, of course".

After we had kissed and cuddled, Geno asked if I would mind going with him to the Curry's PC World. "Oh Geno", I said; "Surely you are satisfied with being a successful caterer and businessman? I know that you've got a big truncheon, but why do you want to be a policeman as well? And why are the police eating curries anyway?" "No Jim", he replied, "you misunderstand. It is the big electrical shop. I just need to get a few bits for the café. We could take the train over there for a change, if you like. There's no rush; it is open quite late". "Oh lovely", I said; "It sounds like me: open all hours".

We went over to Blundellsands station to catch the train. Taking the train made a nice change from the ice cream van. We held hands and watched the scenery go by. We cuddled up in the dark tunnels. "Oh Geno", I said; "I love it when you come down my tunnels like this".

To get to the big shops at Aintree, we needed to change trains at Sandhills station. The station was packed with lads getting off to catch the bus to the football match. "Do you follow the football much?", Geno asked me. "Not really, mate", I said, "although I do really appreciate the beauty of footballers. I love to see them dribble at the front. And, of course, I really appreciate good ball control and great tackle. Tell me, Geno, do you support Roma?" I had inadvertently committed a cardinal sin. "Roma?!", he said; "Certainly not! I support Lazio. We are bitter rivals, just like your Liverpool and Netherton". "Everton, love", I gently corrected him; "I am sorry, I hope I didn't offend you. I think my city has quite friendly rivalry, though. You know, we always keep a sense of humour. And it's good to appreciate both colours – red and blue. After all, Geno, you make me red hot when I'm with you, and I feel blue when we are apart". "That's sweet", he said.

So we caught the other train going up to Aintree, and after a few stops we soon arrived. "I bet you feel right at home here in Aintree, Geno", I said. "Why's that?", he asked. "Well, mate", I continued, "I think you're the only man I know who has had more jumps than the Grand National".

It was mad busy inside the electrical shop. There was one guy at the service desk complaining that he was having trouble with his X Box. "It's knackered", he said; "It keeps getting a red ring". I know that feeling. By the time I get a red ring, I'm usually ready for a kip too.

"So, tell me Geno, what are you looking for here?", I asked. "Well, I've got my eye on a little chopper", he replied. "Oh, I bet you have!", I said. "No", continued Geno, "I mean a Braun multi-quick blender. It would really help with the milkshakes. Come on, let's go and have a look".

There were rows of small appliances to look through and we enjoyed having a browse. Geno was very taken with the electric juicers. "This would be perfect", he said; "Look, it let's you squeeze every last drop of juice out!" "You normally don't have any trouble doing that!", I said. Next we found a small vibrating whisk. My imagination started to run away with me when I thought about what we could do with that, but Geno explained it was for frothing the cappuccinos. A sales assistant recommended that we have a look at the new coffee machine models. "They're great", she said; "Just look at these big jugs!" "Thank you", I said, "but big jugs are not really my cup of tea".

Finally Geno found what he was looking for. He was so excited to get his hands on a big chopper. You should have seen all the attachments! You could chop, blend, pulse and smooth. Now that's the sort of chopper you want to have in your hands! Geno was happily musing about all the lovely milkshakes and fruit smoothies he could make. It was lovely to see how a big chopper could bring a smile to his face.

Later, Geno asked if we could take a look at the hoovers. "Certainly", I said, "you know how much I enjoy a bit of suction!" There was plenty of choice to look through, a really good selection of suction devices. "Look at all the settings on this one!", I exclaimed; "Lino, parquet, short loop. And I think this would be my favourite setting: deep shag!" "Oh Jim", he said; "I think these refer to different types of flooring. I think it is a type of carpet, you know, deep shag pile". "Oh my goodness, Geno", I said; "I really didn't know that shagging too deeply could give you piles! Still, I suppose that would explain a few things".

I was feeling tired after looking round the shop, so I had a little sit down in a chair that they had on the side. I couldn't help noticing that the chair seemed to be plugged in and had buttons and knobs on the side. "Oh my goodness", I thought to myself; "Surely we haven't started using electric chairs in the UK? Surely that is more of an American thing?" But you know me; I never could resist twiddling a knob. So I pressed the power on button and started fiddling with the settings. Before long I felt strong, firm nobbles penetrating my back. Not for the first time in my life, I must admit. I felt these nobbles massaging my aching muscles. I began to feel more and more relaxed. I let out a contented sigh. I think I must have drifted off to sleep.

I was rudely awakened from my slumbers by a security guard. He prodded me and said, "Excuse me, sir; I'm sorry to disturb you". "Don't worry mate", I replied; "I'm already disturbed". He poked me again (not in a good way). Honestly, the shame of being manhandled by a store detective, when I hadn't even nicked anything. "I'm sorry to disturb you, sir", he repeated, "but I had to wake you as it is 6.50 p.m. and the store will be closing soon". I thanked him for kindly arousing me in such a considerate manner. "Now, where has Geno got to?", I wondered to myself.

Just then, Geno strode up carrying a beautifully wrapped box. "Jim", he said; "I've got a little something for you". "Believe me, love", I said, "you've got quite a big something for me". "No", Geno went on, "I mean I've got you a gift", and he handed me his box. "Oh Geno", I gushed, "For me? You shouldn't have gone to so much trouble. It's very kind of you. May I unwrap you, er, I mean unwrap it?" "Yes, of course", smiled Geno; "You can help yourself to my package any time". I eagerly unwrapped Geno's package to find a shiny new laptop inside. "Oh Geno", I said, "it's lovely. You shouldn't have gone to all that expense. And pink too, my favourite colour". "Well, I wanted you to have something nice to help you with writing your diary and book", said Geno. "Thank you so much, love", I said; "You have digitally enhanced me! And I could really do with some enhancements, believe me. I will think of you, Geno, every time I use it". "Yes I hope you will!", said Geno; "Just check out the wallpaper!" "Oh, love, I think you're in the wrong shop for wallpaper. You want B&Q over the other side". "No, love", Geno explained, "the wallpaper is the background picture on the screen. Look!" He powered up the laptop and before long a very sexy picture of a shirtless Geno popped up on the screen. "Oh Geno", I teased, pretending to be shocked; "You promised me faithfully that you were giving up the glamour-modelling. But there you are, bold as brass!" "Well, you know how it is", Geno explained; "You have to keep your hand in". "You can keep your hand in anything you like", I said; "You just help yourself". But that is typical Geno for you; always popping up when you least expect it.

I kissed Geno and thanked him again for the lovely gift, then we left to get the train back home. It was so exciting to get the train. Just think: two rides on Geno's engine in one day!

Saturday 10th October 2015.

I've been really enjoying using my new laptop. I have started typing up some of my old diary entries, and I might even put them together into a book one day. The only problem is that it crashes sometimes. Honestly, sometimes that laptop is up and down. Up and down. It's just like a wild night with Geno. Geno says it's no problem, though; he says if it goes down, you just reboot it and it pops up again. I wish; that really doesn't happen when you get to my age. Still, I must admit, it's wonderful to see Geno's naked torso pop up on the screen when the laptop restarts. You just have to double-click on the picture to make it bigger. If only that worked in real life.

This morning Geno asked me if I had anything on this evening. "Well hopefully I'll have you on top of me with a bit of luck", I replied. "No love", Geno explained; "I meant are you free this evening?". "Free?!", I said indignantly; "Do you mind? I'm a professional! I normally charge a lot. But for a special guy like you I'm willing to waive the charges". Exasperated, poor Geno said, "Jim, let me put it another way; would you like to go to dinner this evening? I'd like to fill you up". "Yes please, baby", I said; "You can fill me up any time you like. I'm available to go out with you anytime. You know I'll always drop anything for you. Especially my pants".

Later on, we jumped in the shower to get ready for our evening out. I was singing away as usual. "You have a good voice there, Jim", Geno said; "I think you have a tenor voice". "Don't be daft, mate", I said; "It's not worth a quid, never mind a tenner!"

We got dressed and headed out. "Let's take the train to town", Geno said. "Oh Geno", I said; "The train again. This will be the third time you've come down my tunnels. I am a very lucky boy!" When we arrived in town, Geno asked if we should have a quick coffee first. We passed by a Costa Coffee shop and Geno asked me if I'd like a quick drink. "Lovely", I said, "but do you mind if we sit outside? I get a bit costaphobic in those places".

Once we had something hot inside us, we set out on a stroll to find somewhere to eat. We walked through the Queen Square (very appropriate, I thought) and Geno spotted Nando's. "Shall we go in here?", he asked. "Well Geno", I said; "I'm sure that you spotted the big cock on the sign outside, but I'm afraid that doesn't directly translate to what's on offer on the menu. It's mainly chicken to eat".

"Oh right", said Geno, "so it might not be the best choice for vegetarians. I am sorry". "Oh don't worry about me", I said; "You know me, Geno; I'll always find something to nibble on".

"Hey Jim, you're a big Abba fan, aren't you?", asked Geno. "Yes, love", I replied; "Why do you ask?" "Well I think Abba loved Nando's", Geno said. "Did they, love?", I asked; "I don't think so". "Yes they did", Geno insisted; "They sang that song, 'For Nando's'". "Oh, Geno, love", I explained, "I think that was called 'Fernando'". "Well", Geno continued, "there was that other song about them being chicken-eaters". "Erm, Geno, I think that one was called 'Chiquitita'", I gently explained.

This conversation was getting way too weird, so we decided to pass on Nando's and look for a bite to eat somewhere else. "I've got a good idea", said Geno; "I know a great Chinese". "Wonderful", I said; "What's his name?" "No", Geno continued, "I mean a Chinese restaurant. Do you fancy a spring roll?" "Why wait for spring, love?", I replied; "I fancy a roll with you anytime".

We arrived at the Chinese restaurant and were seated. "Would you like a drink, Jim?", Geno asked. "Oh, yes please, love", I said; "I could really do with a stiff one". "Well, they do all kinds in here", Geno explained; "They even do cocktails. You can have a Slow Comfortable Screw, or perhaps you would prefer Sex on the Beach?" "Oh no love, thank you", I replied; "I still haven't recovered from that time in the sand dunes in Freshfield. I had sand everywhere. So much so that all the girls mistook my bits for a nail file. It really put the 'man' into 'manicure', I can tell you". "Are you sure you don't want a cocktail, baby?", Geno asked. "No, thank you angel", I replied; "You know I don't drink very much. I don't want to get too tipsy. I could end up being anyone's. Or more likely being no-one's knowing my luck." "I think you'd be OK, Jim", Geno said; "You can hold your own". "Thanks very much, love", I said, "but I'd much rather hold yours".

After we had decided on drinks and ordered our food, we settled down to chat. "Thank you for inviting me to dinner, Geno", I said; "What's the special occasion?" "Well, I was hoping we could discuss our travel plans a bit. I'm keen to do a bit of travelling and I would love you to come along", Geno explained. "I'd love to come with you Geno", I said; "It would be good for you to have some company. After all, no man is an island. Well, apart from the Isle of Man, obviously. You know I once had a terrible experience on the Isle of Man. I got a bit confused and thought that the Laxey Wheel was like a Ferris wheel, so I hopped on. I got drenched; it was like getting stuck on a rinse cycle in the Liver Launderette. When they finally managed to rescue me, they said I should go and visit Douglas, 'cos that would cheer me up. I was so hoping to meet this cute guy called Douglas, but it turned out to just be a town! Another disappointment!"

"I see", said Geno, looking rather confused; "Well I wasn't really thinking about the Isle of Man so much, but I would like to travel a bit around Europe maybe next year. Would you be up for that?" "Oh yes", I said; "I'm very continental. I mean, you'll often see me nibbling on a Toblerone". "And of course, I'd love to show you Italy", Geno continued; "The weather is beautiful. In some parts it is even warm enough to go on the nudist beaches in the autumn and winter". "Oh no, Geno", I said, horrified, "no nudist beaches please. I really haven't got the credentials for that! Naturism has never really appealed to me. I think it would be awkward if we went to the supermarket; believe me, the poor checkout girl would be confused as she wouldn't know if I had three items or less!"

"Have you got any plans for Christmas, Jim?", Geno asked. "Oh, not really", I said; "Christmas can be a bit of a disappointment. Every year I pray that a sexy Santa will come and empty his sack for me. I always hope that a sexy Santa will slide down my chimney, which is always available, let me tell you. I mean, why wait for Christmas Eve? I always try to get into the Christmas spirit, but somehow I just can't get the lid off the bottle". "Well maybe this Christmas will be different", Geno said; "You have me now", and he gently kissed me. "Thank you, love", I said; "Well yes I suppose Christmas is a time for miracles. I mean, a virgin birth I can believe in, but me finding a boyfriend is a bit harder to swallow. Literally. And what's all that about three wise men visiting? It's taken me all this time to find one wise man". I kissed Geno. "Normally at Christmas, the only thing I can pull is a cracker", I said, "so it is so good to be with you".

"The reason I'm asking about Christmas is that I want this Christmas to be really special", Geno explained; "I really want to give you a big package at Christmas, Jim". "Oh Geno", I said, "there's no need for that, love. You give me a big package every night". "Jim, I'd really like to go to Rome for Christmas, if possible", said Geno; "I would be honoured if you would come with me". "Oh Geno, I'd love to", I said; "It would be a dream come true. I have wanted to visit Rome for ages. I never thought I would have the chance to go, and I never thought I would be able to share the experience with someone I loved". "Well, I think it would be the perfect trip for us", Geno said. "Yes indeed", I agreed; "A trip to the eternal city to celebrate our eternal love".

"Do you remember me mentioning my sister Serena?", Geno asked. "Yes, love", I said; "She's a cook at the Vatican, isn't she?" "Yes, darling, that's right. And she's pregnant. She's due to give birth around Christmas time, and that's the main reason I would like to go home for Christmas". "Oh Geno, that's wonderful", I said; "You're going to be an uncle!". "Yes, I can't wait", Geno said; "Serena has had her scan and already knows that she is having a boy, so I'm going to have a nephew!" "Oh Geno, that will be wonderful", I said; "I bet you will spoil him rotten". "Yes", agreed Geno; "When he gets a bit older, I don't think he will ever be short of ice cream! You know, my sister is very independent and strong. She is determined to have a natural childbirth, without medical intervention. Ideally she wants to have a water-birth in the Trevi fountain". "Blimey, Geno", I said, "I can't imagine what it must be like for a woman to be in labour. If I was in that situation, I don't think I would be brave enough to have a natural childbirth. No, I think I would be asking the medics for everything they had, you know: peppermint, equinox and an epidermis. But I guess men and women are different, and they can cope with different things." "Yes indeed", Geno said; "You know what they say, 'men are from Mars and women are from Venus'". "Yes", I agreed; "And gay men are from Uranus".

"I hope that my brother Antonio may be able to get us an audience with the Pope when we visit Rome", Geno said. "Oh yes, Geno, that would be wonderful", I agreed. "You know you have to kneel down and kiss his ring", Geno explained. "Right, love", I said; "Well I'd better get practising. You know, Christmas is only a couple of months away. I'd better get organised. I haven't renewed my passport, so I need to get cracking on that. It's so expensive, but I met this guy down the market who said he can make passports for £20 so I might give that a go".

We had a lovely meal, and happily chatted about our plans to visit Rome. When we had finished, we walked back to Central Station to get the train back to Blundellsands & Crosby. Have you seen those new hologram assistants they have in the station? Very freaky. That poor woman has been stood still in the same position for at least 6 weeks to my knowledge. Just as I went through the ticket barrier, she piped up: "Please don't take heavy and bulky items on the escalators. It is much safer to use the lift for heavier items". I was mortified. Was she talking to me? Honestly, I've only been for one Chinese meal; I have not put on that much weight!

The train arrived and we were soon back in Blundellsands. I couldn't wait to cuddle up with Geno and to happily fall asleep to dream about our very own Roman holiday.

Saturday 17th October 2015.

I woke up this morning and thought I'm going to have to bite the bullet. I'm really going to have to get my passport renewed. I've just had my payday, so I can't put off getting my passport any longer. Each payday I hope and pray that there will be a few extra zeroes on the amount. The problem is that the zeroes are always at the front of the number and not at the end. Now the first thing to do, of course, is to get some photos taken.

I went to have a look in the mirror and was a bit shocked by what I saw. Not exactly photogenic. More sort of phototoxic really. So, I got out my best slap and set about a bit of resurfacing work. A dab of concealer always helps to hide a multitude of sins. A little foundation base helps to even things out. And of course a little powder helps to finish your look and blurs things nicely. After a few minutes I looked almost human, and so I dared to venture out to town. Geno said he would come with me too as he needed to do a bit of shopping.

When we arrived in town, Geno kindly walked with me to the photo shop so that I could get my passport photos taken, before he left to do a bit of shopping. "I'll see your bits, Jim", he said. "Geno, love", I said, "you've already seen my bits many times. We normally say, 'I'll see you in a bit'". "Yes, that's it", said Geno; "See you and your bits". And with that he kissed me briefly and hurried off.

The assistant in the photo shop was a formidable woman who was very efficient and forthright. She explained to me that the most important thing was not to smile when having my photo taken. I didn't think there was any danger of me smiling. To be honest, I had put on so much anti-ageing serum this morning that I could hardly move my facial muscles at all. She stood me in front of a white screen and continued to bark out orders: "Take your glasses off! Don't blink! Close your mouth! Don't smile! Keep your eyes open! Now get ready, I'm going to shoot!" I prayed that she meant with a camera and not with a weapon. I wondered how she came to be working in a photo shop. I couldn't imagine how she could possibly have failed the recruitment tests for the SS. Still, it was all over fairly quickly (the story of my life), and she assured me that the results would cut the mustard at the passport office. So I paid, said thank you and left quickly (again, the story of my life).

I gave Geno a quick buzz on my phone to see where he was and where we could meet up. There seemed to be a man's voice in the background asking about ring sizes. "How impertinent!", I thought; "Geno's ring size is my business and no-one else's!". Geno asked me to meet him outside Debenhams in a few minutes.

I waited for Geno for a while outside Debenhams. He came up after a while and I kissed him. "Have you had a good time, love?", I asked; "Have you been looking at anything nice?". "Yes, very nice", Geno replied enigmatically.

"So what do you want from Debenhams?", I asked Geno. "Oh, I'm just looking for a few presents to take home to my family", he replied; "For example, my sister wants a John Rocha bag for £100". "Blimey, Geno, £100!", I said; "That's crazy! Especially when you think you can get a John Lewis bag for 5p".

We had a good look around Debenhams. Geno managed to drag me away from the Clinique counter so that he could focus on choosing Christmas presents for his family. Afterwards, Geno asked me to accompany him to a music shop. He said that he was going to play 'The Magic Flute' for me. Honestly, in broad daylight! I just hoped that he was talking about Mozart, and that 'The Magic Flute' was not a euphemism for something else.

I really enjoyed Geno's company, and we had a great time going around town. When Geno had got all of his gifts sorted, we happily set off back to Blundellsands. On our return to the flats, we saw that the postman had been, and indeed Geno's box was stuffed full (not for the first time). He sifted through his letters and came across one with an Italian stamp. As he opened it and read the contents, I could see the colour drain from his face. His eyes seemed to turn worried as he turned from me and stuffed the letter into his pocket. "What's the matter, love?", I asked gently.

Chapter 8.

Saturday 28th November 2015.

"It's not long now till we fly out to Rome, my love!", Geno said. "Yes indeed, angel", I replied; "It's been a long time coming. I can't wait!". "Are you looking forward to seeing your family again, baby?", I asked. Geno answered, "Yes, I am", but his eyes betrayed a tinge of sadness. I couldn't help thinking about that letter he got from Italy, last month. When I asked him about it, he said it was from his brother Dario. I had asked Geno if the letter contained bad news. He answered 'no', and assured me that everyone was safe and well, but mentioned that Dario had heard from one of Geno's old friends who wanted to meet him when he was next in Rome. "But surely that's a good thing?", I had said to him; "It would be nice to catch up with old friends". "Well", Geno had replied at the time, "we had quite a lot of history". I hadn't asked further questions as I sensed that Geno wasn't comfortable talking about it. I just gently reminded him that I was there for him if he ever needed to talk, but he had not talked about it any further.

Well, whatever it is that has been upsetting Geno, I just hope that I can help him through it. And I hope that it doesn't spoil our trip too much. I hope that things will work themselves out. And speaking of workouts, I'd better get going as Geno has promised to give me a bench press in the gym. Well, he's welcome to press anything he wants, let's be honest. He also said that I need to do lots of squats and lunges in the gym, so that sounds promising. Sometimes I don't see the attraction of the gym. I mean who wants to be stuck in a room filled with sweaty, groaning men? Oh, hang on a minute...

Friday 18th December 2015.

Before Geno and I set off on our trip to Rome, I wanted to visit my dear friend Vincent to say 'goodbye'. Vin is a wonderful guy; so clever and talented. He works in cardiology, so it will come as no surprise when I tell you that he has healing hands. And he has a wonderful bedside manner; he always warms his hands first. I think it is very appropriate that he works in cardiology healing hearts. Mind you, he is so good-looking that I reckon he must break a few hearts too! And he's a wonderfully gifted musician. You should hear him playing the violin. Yes, he's always on the fiddle. But I've told him that there's no point being on the fiddle all the time; honestly, he's going to have to pay his taxes sometime. Really, I wish I had known him back in the day when I had my first flat and needed to break into the lecky meter. I don't mind telling you that if I wasn't with Geno then I would be more than happy to have Vin caress my strings with his bow! It's wonderful to watch him unpacking his instrument.

So, I arranged to go round to Vin's flat to catch up and have a proper chat before we left for Italy. When I arrived, one of his friends had popped in for coffee, but Vin was running short of milk. I offered to pop over the road to get some milk from the shop. "Do you have skimmed milk or semi-skimmed?", I asked. "Oh no, I always have full-fat milk", the stunning hunk replied. "Vin!", I exclaimed; "Please may I remind you that you work in cardiology on the heart ward? You need to set an example!" "Oh, it's OK", he replied; "We always give the patients full-fat milk, Jim". "Blimey, mate", I said; "What else do you give them? Ciggies and bacon butties?!" Personally, I always go for semi-skimmed. Well you know me; it seems that I've always got a semi.

When I got back from the shop, we settled down to tea and coffee and Vin very kindly filled me in on all the best sights to see while in Rome. "You must see the beautiful statues and spend time gazing at the exquisite busts", he said. "Oh, so you've met Geno then?", I replied. "And don't forget the Spanish Steps", Vin kindly continued. "Thanks, mate", I replied, "but I think I'll give that a miss. I'm really not good at dancing". Before I left, Vin kindly wished me a safe and happy trip. I promised to send him a postcard from the Vatican post office. Knowing my luck, a stamp will be the only thing I get to lick.

Tuesday 22nd December 2015.

"Have you stuffed everything in yet, Jim?", Geno asked. I blushed, and said, "I beg your pardon, love?" "I mean, have you finished packing?", Geno said; "We have to be at the airport for 3pm." "Yes, love", I said, "I think I'm done. I've packed my passport, plenty of clothes and, most importantly, plenty of make-up. I was rushin' round the shops yesterday getting all my bits. You know me, always rushin' here and rushin' there. Honestly, you might as well call me Vladimir and pour me a vodka, I've been rushin' round that much. I made sure that I got plenty of cream from Boots too, 'cos my eczema is really playing up. Honestly, I don't think my stomach will ever be like a washboard; it's more like an emery board.

"It's good that you're packed love", Geno said; "Did you remember to get some currency?". "Well, yes", I replied; "I went into the Post Office and asked for some *lire*. But they said they didn't do those anymore and I could only have these Euro things instead. I was so excited 'cos I thought they meant tickets to the Eurovision Song Contest. But when they passed the Euros over, they didn't look like tickets, so I left them". "Oh Jim!", Geno exclaimed; "Euros are the currency we use in Italy nowadays. We haven't used *lire* for some years now. You should have bought some notes. Never mind, we can get some at the airport. Come on, let's get ready to go".

I took one last lingering look at Geno's beautiful torso as he grabbed a checked shirt and slipped it on. "That's a lovely shirt, Geno", I said; "I wish I could wear checks like that. The problem when I wear checks is that the checks always bounce. I'll never forget that time when my cheque bounced in Specsavers and they sent the lads round to repossess my varifocals. I was mortified".

We grabbed our bags and put them by the door, ready to go. We stroked and petted Clara, and then Geno popped next door to leave his keys with a kind neighbour who had kindly offered to pop in to feed Clara and keep an eye on her while we were away. When Geno came back he took one last look around the flat. He stood for a moment and gazed out of the window, surveying the beach and the Irish Sea beyond. I thought I detected a small tear in the corner of his eye, so I went up to him to hug and kiss him. "Are you OK, love?", I asked. "Oh, I'm fine", he replied; "I'm just feeling a bit emotional about seeing my family again". "Well then", I said, "don't be standing there, looking like one of Lewis's! We've got a plane to catch!". "Come on then", Geno replied, picking up the bags; "Wow Jim, you've got a lot of baggage!". "Yes, you're not the first man who has said that to me", I replied; "Oh, right, I see what you mean. I have tried to travel light, but you know how it is – a boy has clothes!'.

Once we had gathered our bags together and locked the flat up, we walked over to Blundellsands station to catch the train into town. I was so excited to be going on holiday, I could hardly contain myself. I cuddled up close to Geno on the train. "When was the last time that you took a holiday, Jim?", Geno asked. I had to think about this for a moment as I really couldn't remember. "Erm, I'm not very good at taking holidays or days off", I explained; "You know what work is like; there's never a good time to have it off".

On arrival in town, we walked the short distance to Lime Street station to catch the train to Manchester Airport. It all felt so real now. I was so excited to be embarking on this trip. It really was a dream come true to be able to visit Rome, and to be able to share the experience with the man of my dreams, well, that really did make the dream a reality.

When we arrived at Manchester Airport, I was quivering with anticipation. I just couldn't wait to get on the plane. We went to the check-in desk first of all. The check-in clerk at the desk was gorgeous. "Here we go", Geno said, "he will check us in". "I'd rather check him out, to be honest", I said. "Hello", I said to the check-in clerk as we passed over our passports and placed our bags on the scales. "Good morning, sir", the check-in clerk replied; "Now did you pack these bags yourself?". "Oh yes", I replied; "It took me hours. And I packed Geno's, too. He needs a bit of mothering, you know". "I see", said the clerk; "And have you left them unattended at all? Could anyone have slipped something in without your knowledge?" "Oh, no", I said, "certainly not! I'm very vigilant about that sort of thing".

Once we had got our boarding cards, we headed over to passport control. The security guy was even more gorgeous. Absolutely stunning, to be honest. "Geno!", I said; "Check him out! He's gorgeous!" "Yes", agreed Geno; "He's built like a rugby player". "Indeed he is", I said; "Well I wouldn't mind getting into a scrum with him! I bet his tackle is fantastic! Mind you, with rugby players you have to watch out for oddly-shaped balls". My mind went into panic mode. "How can I make sure that the alarm goes off so that he has to search me?", I wondered to myself. I thought about leaving my watch on, but it's mainly made of plastic. And I don't have metal-rimmed glasses any more. There was only one thing for it. I took my keys and quickly stuffed them down my pants while no-one was looking. As I approached passport control the cute security guy asked me to empty my pockets. "Certainly", I said, "I'd be happy to empty anything for you. I placed my phone and wallet in a tray so that I could go through the scanner. As expected the alarm duly beeped, and I feigned embarrassment. "Would you step forward please, sir?", the gorgeous security guard said; "Please stand with your arms out and your legs spread apart". "Oh, you know me so well", I giggled; "Should I strip off ready for a full body search?" "I don't think that will be necessary, sir", he replied as he systematically felt along my outstretched limbs. Finding nothing of particular interest, he started going over me with his hand-held scanner. I began to regret my actions when the scanner started buzzing as he hovered it around my crotch. I was so embarrassed. I was mortified. "Sir", the security guard said, "you appear to have a metal item down your trousers. I have to ask you if you have a pistol in your pants?" "Hardly!", Geno exclaimed. I scowled at Geno. "No", I explained to the security guy, "I haven't got a gun down my trousers. I think I might have dropped my keys down my pants". "I see", said the security guy; "May I ask why?". I blushed. I really couldn't think of a credible explanation. Fortunately Geno came to my rescue. "Well I bought Jim this lovely keyring, you see", he said; "He was worried about pickpockets, so he placed it in his pants". "I see, sir", said the handsome security guy; "Well if I could please ask you to remove the keys from your pants so that you can pass through passport control correctly I would be very grateful". I was so embarrassed, but I had brought it on myself. I wriggled and managed to get my keys out so that I could pass through the scanner without any alarms going off. Once we had passed through, Geno told me off. "Honestly, Jim", he said, "I can't take you anywhere!". "Of course you can, love", I replied; "You can take me any place you like".

As we had a bit of time before boarding the plane, Geno suggested that we take a look at the duty free. There were dozens of bottles of aftershaves. It was really good fun to experiment with the different fragrances. You know me, I always enjoy a little squirt of something fresh and fruity. Geno was checking out all the drinks. "Wow look at all these", he said; "They've got all kinds of spirits and liqueurs". "Liqueurs indeed!", I said; "Oh Geno, I'd much rather lick yours!"

Finally it was time to board the plane and we were called to the gate. I was so excited to be jetting off with my wonderful Geno. As we went through the boarding gate and onto the plane, I couldn't have felt happier. We found our seats and settled down, cuddled up together, ready for the adventure to begin. The flight attendants were very, well, attentive. "Are you OK fastening your seatbelt and getting it nice and tight?", one of them asked me. "Oh yes", I answered cheerily; "I'm an expert. I never miss a Thursday night at the fetish club".

They gave the safety briefing, and I sat with baited breath as the plane began to taxi to the runway. Geno held my hand and whispered, "Just take a deep breath and relax, baby. I'll take you higher than you've ever been before". "Hmm, promises, promises", I replied. As the plane turned to straighten up at the end of the runway, the engines began to roar as we prepared for take-off. This was it, the point of no return. No turning back now. I held Geno's hand tightly and kissed him tenderly as we shot up into the sky.

Once we had completed our ascent, I felt much calmer and less nervous when we were cruising at altitude. Not that I'm the sort of guy to go cruising; you know what I mean. It's wonderful when you're up there in the air; beautiful blue skies above the clouds, above the weather, like being in a perfect world. The flight was smooth, no turbulence, thank goodness. Geno appreciated this particularly, saying "I like a smooth flight. There's nothing worse than a rough passage". "Tell me about it", I said.

I felt so contented, sitting there next to Geno. "I love you, darling", I said as I kissed him; "You have awoken these strong feelings and deep emotions within me". "Me too", Geno replied; "I'm feeling something deep inside". "Yeah", I said, "not for the first time, I'll bet".

After a while, the flight attendants brought round the drinks. You know the trolley was like Geno on roller skates – hot stuff on wheels. "Can I get you anything, sir?", the attendant asked Geno. "Well yes please", Geno replied; "I would really like a black Americano". "Wouldn't we all mate?", I said; "Do you mind, love, there's a queue here. And if there are any hot black Americans to be had, then I'm first in line!". Geno shot me a quizzical look. Well, suffice to say Geno had been talking about coffee, and he got a steaming cup while I opted for an orange juice. We sipped away happily. "Would you like more juice, angel?", Geno asked me. "Oh yes please, love", I said; "You know me; I always like to squeeze out the last drop".

Before we knew it, there was an announcement that we were about to make our descent into Leonardo da Vinci – Fiumicino Airport. "Oh isn't that sweet?", I said to Geno; "They have named the airport after the teenage mutant ninja turtles". Geno seemed to put his head down in shame. I'm not sure why. But thank God we had a safe landing and were soon disembarking in Rome. It was pleasantly mild as we stepped off the plane and headed into the terminal building. We went over to the carousels to collect our bags. "Jim, I still don't understand why you have to carry so much baggage", Geno said. "Well", I replied, "you know how it is, love. I'm Catholic".

We were met at the airport by Geno's brother, Dario, who had kindly come to collect us. Dario embraced Geno and me warmly, and then kindly drove us over to their family home in Castel Gandolfo. Our Italian adventure was just about to begin.

Wednesday 23rd December 2015.

I had a lovely breakfast with Geno and his family at their home this morning. Geno's mum seemed to have difficulty remembering my name, and so he introduced me again. "Mama", he said, "this is my boyfriend, Jim". "Tim?", she replied. "No, Mama, Jim". "Vin?", she asked. "Jim". "Glynn?" "Blimey, Geno", I said; "How many fellas have you got on the go?! This is like the litany of the saints!"

After breakfast, Dario kindly said he would drop Geno and me off in Rome so that we could explore the city. I was so excited. There was history everywhere you looked. You can see why people say that Rome wasn't built in a day! First up was the magnificent Coliseum. It was amazing to see it in real life. You could just feel the history and imagine the Emperor and the Crystal Virgins sitting in the box watching the Gladiators battle it out. The Gladiators indeed! Honestly, I didn't even know they had TVs in Roman times!

Then Geno said he would go down (I wish) and show me the *hypogeum*. Geno explained that it was like an underground labyrinth or maze beneath the arena where gladiators and animals waited before the contests began. "Ooh, a maze!", I said; "Perhaps we could play hide and seek! Gay men are always good at hide and seek. They usually know who is coming up behind them".

After a fascinating exploration of the Coliseum, Geno suggested a little lunch. "I know a great restaurant", he said; "Do you think you could manage the Spanish Steps?" "I'll try, love", I said, "although when you get to my age, I wish they would install a Spanish Escalator". "How do you feel about antipasto, Jim?", he asked me. "How could anyone be anti-pasta?", I said; "I love pasta! I mean take spaghetti for example, it starts off straight but once it gets all hot and steamy it goes really bent. Come to think of it, I know a few people like that". "No love, not anti-pasta. It's called antipasto", Geno explained; "It's like a starter, a platter to share. I think you would like the mushrooms and artichokes. I can ask them to take the meat out for you". "Oh Geno", I said, "I always get so sad when you take your meat out".

After lunch, Geno informed me that he had a real treat for me this afternoon – a visit to the Vatican. I was so excited as I had wanted to visit the Vatican for years. We started off in St. Peter's Square. The beautiful Christmas tree and crib scene were delightful. It was fascinating to see the obelisk; it was really wonderful to see such a magnificent erection up close. Then, Geno said he would take me round the back entrance to get into the Vatican museums. "They're wonderful", he enthused, "and it includes a visit to the Sistine Chapel". "Oh, I would love to see the Sixteenth Chapel", I said; "I can't wait to check out Mike and Angelo's handiwork".

We joined the queue at the entrance to the Vatican Museums and paid our entrance fee. I was amazed by everything I saw. I loved the Bramante staircase, the beautiful iron double spiral staircase designed by Momo. "Blimey, Geno", I said; "I wonder what they had been drinking when they designed this staircase? I hope I don't fall!". "Don't worry, darling", Geno replied, "I'll catch you".

As we went through the museums, I loved seeing all the portraits and statues. And the Popemobiles were fascinating. But of course the gruel in the frown was the Sixteenth Chapel at the end. It was simply magnificent. I was in awe of the beautiful frescoes and history. "The frescoes are stunning", Geno said. "Yes indeed, love", I replied; "You are spoiling me with these frescoes. Most of the time I'm only used to seeing Tesco's". "You can just imagine the cardinals marching in solemn procession into the Chapel to elect a new Pope", Geno explained; "They get locked in the Chapel until they have elected the new Pope. Then the smoke goes up the chimney". "Well, love, I wouldn't mind being locked in with you for a bit", I said, "but I really didn't know that the cardinals were all into chain-smoking".

After a wonderful look around the Vatican museums, we headed back round to St. Peter's Square. We walked up towards the steps of St. Peter's Brazilians (sorry, Basilica; Geno corrected me). "Would you like to meet a Swiss guard?", Geno asked, gesturing towards one of the guardsmen on duty by the entrance to the Basilica. "That would be nice, love", I said, "although I would quite like to meet a Swiss roll. I'm starving again!". "Oh, what are you like?", Geno said; "Didn't you have enough lunch, Jim?" "Well", I explained, "it's not easy nibbling on mushrooms, you know. It can be very difficult getting your lips around those big heads". Anyway, we went up to chat to the Swiss guard, and he was really nice. He told us all about his work and how the guards swore to protect the Pope. He explained that all of the guards were indeed from Switzerland and Catholics and unmarried; fit young men who lived in a barracks here at the Vatican. I glanced at Geno and exchanged smiles. Things were certainly looking up! So, there was a barracks full of unmarried fit young men, all cramped together in an all-male environment! Why don't they tell you this sort of thing in the guide books?! They'd have people flocking from all over the world.

Eventually we managed to tear ourselves away from the handsome Swiss guard and we went into the Basilica. It was stunning. I especially loved seeing Mike and Angelo's *Pietà*. It was such a beautiful sculpture. Geno recommended that we go up to the top of the dome as the view of Rome was stunning from there. "Oh Geno", I said, "it seems awfully personal having a peek under Mike and Angelo's dome. I hope they don't mind!"

We started to climb the stairs up to the top of the dome of St. Peter's. Did you know that there were 551 steps up to the top? Well, I do now! I wish I had taken my inhaler with me; I was gasping by the top. But the view was simply stunning. I held Geno close and kissed him tenderly as we gazed out across the Roman skyline. "I love you, darling", Geno whispered; "I want you to be mine". "No problem", I replied; "You can have me any time you like. Please just help yourself".

Strange how it was quicker going down the stairs than it was going up. And then Geno informed me that there was a lift which could have taken us part of the way up! I was fuming! My asthma can be quite bad and so I would have been grateful for a lift. There's nothing worse than being out of breath; I can't tell you how many times people have hung up on me on the phone because they thought I was doing heavy breathing. Still, I couldn't stay cross at Geno; I love him far too much to hold a grudge.

When we got back down to ground level, it was almost time for the Mass to begin in the Basilica, so we took our seats. It was so beautiful to hear the choir singing. I just had to join in with the psalms and hymns (there were quite a few 'hims' that I would have liked to join in with too, but I won't go into that). "You've got a great voice, Jim", Geno said; "I think you're a countertenor". "Thanks very much, love", I said, "but I'm sure I can count to more than ten".

After Mass, we met Geno's brother, Antonio, who was on duty patrolling the Basilica. "Welcome to Rome and to the Vatican City State, Jim!", he said; "Now if you will both please follow me, the Holy Father would like to meet you". "I beg your pardon!", I exclaimed; "The Pope would like to meet Geno and me?!" "Well yes", Antonio said, "I've told him all about you". And with that, Antonio led us over to the Santa Marta guest house where the Pope was residing. "Oh my goodness!", I exclaimed; "An audience with the Pope! I feel even more excited than when I watched 'An Audience with Lily Savage'!"

We were taken up to the Pope's apartment, where Antonio introduced us. "Your Holiness", Antonio said, "please may I introduce my brother Geno and his friend Jim". "Welcome, come in", said the Pope, making a very good attempt at speaking in English. I knelt down to kiss his ring as is the custom. The Holy Father greeted Geno first, saying: "How lovely to see you, Geno! Tell me, how is your sister, Serena, doing?" "Very well, Your Holiness", Geno replied; "She is due to give birth to her first child any day now". "How exciting!", said the Pope; "What a wonderful blessing at Christmas time! And this must be your friend Jim". Turning to me, the Pope kindly addressed me: "Jim, I am pleased to meet you. I have heard all about you". I blushed. "Oh, Your Holiness", I explained, "that was all a long time ago when I was an altar boy in Liverpool. I thought it had all been forgotten about. I hope that I have not caused too much embarrassment to the Church". "Erm, I'm not sure what you are talking about, Jim", the Pope said; "It's just that I understand you are a very kind and loving friend of Geno's. And I also wanted to speak with you as I understand you work with domestic appliances".

Well, it was turning out to be a very interesting day. What was going to happen next? Was the Pope going to ask me to fix his cooker? He clarified his intentions: "The thing is, Jim, I am not getting any younger. I may have to start thinking about retiring at some point, and then there will need to be another conclave to elect the new Pope. I want everything to be ready when that time comes". "I see, Your Holiness", I said, "and how can I help you with that?" "Well, I understand that you deal with gas fires, Jim", the Pope said, "and I was thinking of installing a new fire in the Sistine Chapel all ready for the smoke to rise to give the joyous news of the election of the new Pope. Perhaps you can show me some models?" "Erm, certainly", I replied, whipping out my phone and showing off some models from the website. I mean models of fires. I don't mean male models. Oh, you know what I mean. The Pope seemed to particularly like the larger fires called the 'Straight' and 'Relaxed' fires. I must be honest, the names of these fires have always made me laugh over the years; I think because 'straight' and 'relaxed' are two adjectives that will probably never describe me very well.

I felt sure that the fire installation in the Sistine Chapel would not be successful, but when you are dealing with the Pope you have to be tactful. "Your Holiness", I began, "the thing is that the ceiling of the Sistine Chapel is very high. It must be over 20 metres tall. That is probably too long a chimney to get rid of the smoke effectively. The smoke could back up, and billow into the Chapel, damaging the beautiful frescoes". "I see", said the Pope, looking rather disappointed. "And surely", I went on, "you wouldn't want to have the cardinals poking about in your flue when you have a blockage?" "No, of course not", said the Pope. "Well then, Your Holiness, please let me find you a more suitable stove to put into the Chapel", I suggested. "Certainly, Jim; that sounds like a very good proposal! Please could you start work straight after Christmas, before you go back to England?", the Pope asked. "Certainly, Holy Father", I replied; "It will be my pleasure". And with that, we said our goodbyes and withdrew, tenderly kissing the Pope's ring on the exit.

"Wow, Geno; what a day!", I said as we travelled back to Castel Gandolfo. "Yes indeed", agreed Geno, "and it's only the beginning. I've got so much more I want to show you, Jim". "I bet you have!", I said; "Well, you know what they say, I'm in Rome, so I might as well do a Roman!".

Thursday 24th December 2015.

Christmas Eve! I can't believe that Christmas is nearly here!

The day started very busily, as Geno and I helped his mum with a million chores: cleaning, tidying, wrapping presents, putting out the Christmas nativity crib figures and helping to prepare food. By the time we had finished, it was nearly lunch time. Geno suggested that we go out for a walk and to explore the city a bit more, and Dario kindly said that he would give us a lift and drop us in the city to explore a bit further.

When we arrived back in Rome's city centre, Geno asked me what I would like to see next. "There is so much to see in Rome", Geno explained; "So much history, so much culture. I don't know how we are going to squeeze it all in". "Geno, love", I said, "you don't normally have any difficulties in squeezing it all in". "No, I mean that there is so much to see", Geno explained; "It would be good to see the other major basilicas, the Pantheon, the Palatine Hill and the Roman Forum. And it's not just Rome that is worth a visit. When we come again, there are so many places in the country that I would like to show you. I mean, I would love to wake up inside Florence one morning". "Who on earth is Florence, may I ask?!", I said; "I didn't know that you had a penchant for sleeping with women, Geno. Is there something you would like to tell me?" "Don't be silly, Jim", Geno went on; "Florence isn't a woman. It's a city in Tuscany. And we must visit Venice to see the canals one day". "Oh Geno", I said, "we don't have to go all the way to Venice to see canals. We could just take a little day trip to Salford and see the Manchester Ship Canal".

While we were deciding what to see next, we went into a bar for a little drink. I was sticking to soft drinks as usual, but Geno ordered a Corona Fog. "Are we expecting foggy weather?", I asked; "What is a Corona Fog anyway?". "It's just a Corona beer", Geno explained, "but they add a dash of Tequila, a wedge of lime and a little salt. It just gives it a different taste". "Right, I see", I said; "And do you suck through the lime, or squeeze the juice into the bottle?" "Oh, I like to squeeze all the juice out!", Geno explained; "I really enjoy squeezing fruits". I could feel myself going weak at the knees again. When the drinks arrived, Geno asked me if I would like to try a little swig. I found it hard to get any of the beer out past the wedge of lime that was stuck in the neck of the bottle. "You have to suck harder!", Geno explained. "It's all very well for you to say that, Geno", I said; "You've had more practise! Though I must say that I am enjoying sucking on your Corona".

After our little drink, we went to see the Basilica of Saint John Lateran, which was stunning. We followed this with a lovely stroll around a Christmas market. Then Geno took me for a bite of tea at a little restaurant. "It' Christmas Eve, so I really shouldn't eat meat", Geno explained, "but I could really go for a sirloin steak!". "Blimey mate", I said, "I wouldn't mind getting my hands on your loins, sir". "Any time, babe", Geno said, "any time".

As we munched on our tea, we chatted about the upcoming Christmas festivities. "I'm so excited about spending Christmas with you and your family, Geno", I said; "Tell me what are the plans for tomorrow?" "Oh, don't worry about tomorrow's plans just yet", Geno replied; "I'll fill you in later". "I wish you would mate!", I said; "I really hope you do". "Very funny", Geno said; "Would you like some olive oil on your salad, Jim?' "Yes please, love", I said; "I like to see you drizzling from your nozzle".

A couple sat down at the table opposite us and began to peruse the menus. The lady asked the waiter for advice in English: "Could you recommend something for me as I'm a pescatarian?". "Blimey, Geno", I said; "I didn't know that your star sign affected what you ate". "No Jim, she's not talking about her star sign", Geno explained. "Oh right", I said; "So is it her religion that she is talking about?" "No Jim", Geno explained; "She's a pescatarian. I think it means that she eats fish, but she doesn't eat meat". "Oh, right; I see what you mean, Geno", I said; "You mean that she prefers female company". Geno put his head down in his hands and murmured, "Jim, I really can't take you anywhere, can I?" I just smiled and gave him an apologetic look.

"Come on Jim, let's eat up", Geno said; "We need to leave soon to get over to the Vatican. Antonio will be finishing his shift soon, and he will give us a lift back home". So we ate up and settled the bill, then dashed out into the city. I still had a mouthful to swallow as I ran outside; not for the first time, let's be honest.

Travelling back to Castel Gandolfo, I hugged Geno tight. "I'm so excited about my Italian Christmas adventure!", I said. "Yes, my angel", Geno replied, "and we'd better get an early night. Tomorrow is going to be a very busy day! I wonder what *Babbo Natale* will slip into your stocking tonight?" "Well", I replied, "knowing my luck, mate, it will be athlete's foot! Still, I'm really looking forward to tomorrow".

Friday 25th December 2015.

Christmas Day! Merry Christmas to you!!

The day started early (well, Geno always gets me up early, let's be honest). I kissed Geno and wished him a happy Christmas. We exchanged small gifts, mainly aftershaves, as apparently most gift-giving takes place on the Epiphany, twelve days after Christmas. "I'd like to give you another present later, Jim", Geno said as he kissed me tenderly. "Oh my angel", I said, "you have already given me the greatest gift: yourself".

Downstairs, breakfast was in full swing, and it was a very busy scene. Everyone was hugging and wishing one another *"Buon Natale!"* There were lashings of hot coffee on the go, and we enjoyed slices of delicious *Panettone*. Geno explained that we would have to have a fairly quick breakfast as the family would soon be leaving to drive up to Rome for Christmas Mass at the Vatican. Well, not quite everyone.

Serena was very, very heavily pregnant by this point and so she would be staying in the house with her mother and her husband, Stefano.

The rest of us got ready and went outside for the journey to Rome; some in Dario's car, some in Antonio's and some in Rafaella's. We got up to the Vatican and joined the queue to enter St. Peter's. It felt like such a magical morning as I held Geno's hand. Inside the Basilica, the service was full of beautiful music and carols, candles and incense. It all helped to foster the festive spirit. I snuggled up closer to Geno, drinking in the beauty.

Afterwards, Geno's family got ready to travel back to Castel Gandolfo for dinner, but Geno suggested that he and I stay in Rome for a bit to enjoy some time together. "I'll just have a rummage around in the trunk and see what I can pull out", Geno said. "Geno, love", I said, blushing, "I know very well what you've got inside your trunks. There's really no need to pull it out!" "No Jim", Geno explained, "I mean inside the trunk of the car", and he took out a beautiful picnic basket from the boot of Rafaella's car. "Oh Geno, love", I said, "a picnic! How romantic!" With that, we said our goodbyes to Geno's family and set out to explore the city on foot.

Geno took me to some beautiful places. We went for a walk along the banks of the River Tiber. We climbed up the Gianicolo Hill. The view of the Roman skyline was just stunning. We sat down to enjoy our picnic and to enjoy each other's company. "I love you, Geno", I said; "You light up my life. You are my perfect balance". "And I love you, my darling", Geno echoed my sentiments; "You complete me, Jim. You help me to be a better man. I hate it when we are apart, even for a few hours". "That's just how I feel!", I exclaimed; "When we are apart, I feel like half of me is missing. I wish we could be

together forever". "Yes Jim", Geno agreed, "you are my cell-mate".
"Or perhaps your soulmate?", I gently suggested.

When we had finished our picnic, Geno suggested another stroll. "Do
you mind if we go back to the Vatican, Jim?", he asked; "I'd really like
to take you up the dome again". "Wow, you're a smooth-talker,
Geno", I said; "I bet you say that to all the boys!"

When we got back to St. Peter's Basilica, we started the ascent up to
the dome. Fortunately, we took the lift the first part of the way this
time, so the climb was not quite as arduous. We got to the top, and
surveyed the Roman skyline. Geno looked at his watch. "It's four
o'clock in the afternoon, Jim", he said; "That's three o'clock in
England. Time for the Queen's Speech". "Certainly, love", I said;
"What would you like me to say?" "Actually, Jim", he continued, "I
have something that I would like to say to you".

Geno got down on one knee and whipped out a small package from
his pocket. "Geno!", I hissed; "Not here! Honestly, what would the
Pope say?!" But the small package turned out to be not what I was
expecting. Instead it was a small jewellery gift box and Geno opened
it to reveal a beautiful ring, a plain titanium band. It was very simple.
Just like me.

Geno began to speak: "Jim, I love you", he said; "I have loved you
ever since we met. You fill my life with joy and light. You complete
me and fulfil me. Would you do me the honour of marrying me?"
"Oh, Geno", I said, "I'm sorry, I can't marry you. I'm not a registrar,
you see. And who were you thinking of getting married to, anyway?"
"No, Jim, you misunderstand", Geno explained; "I want to get
married to you. I love you. I want to be your husband and give you
my love forever". I was in shock. "Marriage?!", I exclaimed; "You
mean like being joined together in awful deadlock?" "Why ever not,

Jim?", Geno said; "We love each other and we already live together". "Oh Geno", I said; "I'd love to marry you. You don't know how I've longed to have your ring on my finger. It's just that I don't feel that I am good enough for you. I mean, I'm just an ordinary guy". "No Jim", Geno said, "you are extraordinary. You are the most wonderful man I have ever met. You are so kind, caring and genuine. You are the very best; the cream of the crop". "Well, Geno", I replied, "you are very welcome to sample my cream any time you like, you know that".

"So what do you say, Jim?", Geno asked. I thought and prayed for a few moments. "Yes, yes", I managed to say; "I would be honoured to be your husband". We kissed. "Right, that's settled then", Geno said; "I'm so glad that you have agreed to be my fiancé". "Don't be daft", I said; "I look nothing like Beyoncé". "Now", said Geno, "I just want to take a quick snap of your ring to post on Facebook so that all our friends can see it". "Oh my goodness Geno!", I said, "I'll be mortified! Imagine having pictures of my ring plastered all over the internet!"

Just then, Geno's mobile phone rang. He became very excited and explained that it was his brother, Rafaella, on the phone. "Serena has gone into labour!", he said; "Well in fact, she went into labour shortly after we left this morning, but now the contractions are very close together". "Oh my goodness, Geno, why didn't they call us sooner?", I asked. "I'm sorry", explained Geno, "but my family were in on my plan to propose, so they wanted to give us some time together. But Rafaella is on the way over now to collect us and take us back to Castel Gandolfo. We'd better get down the stairs as quickly as we can".

We descended the steps from the dome of St. Peter's back down to ground level, and rushed out into St. Peter's Square to await Rafaella's arrival. We waited 20 to 30 minutes but there was still no sign of him. Geno telephoned Rafaella and discovered that there had been a car crash which was blocking Rafaella from getting into Rome. Nobody had been badly injured, thank goodness, but it was going to take a while for the road to be cleared. "Oh dear", said Geno, "how are we going to get over there now? On Christmas Day as well! I know, I have an idea. There's only one thing for it!" And with that, he went off to speak to a Swiss Guardsman who was on duty in the Square. The Guardsman nodded and walked off, returning a few minutes later with the Pope.

"*Buon Natale*, Your Holiness", I said. "It's lovely to see you both again", the Pope said; "Now, I've just heard the wonderful news that the baby is on the way. Geno, your family does so much to support me, now I want to help if I can. My helicopter is at your disposal to get you back to Castel Gandolfo quickly. Please follow me". The Holy Father and the Swiss Guardsman led us through the beautiful Vatican gardens behind St. Peter's Basilica, to the helicopter landing pad. The pilot was already there and, before we climbed on board, the Pope wished us good luck. "Please give my best wishes to Serena and Stefano", the Pope said; "I can't wait to see the new baby!" We said our thank-yous and Geno made a quick call to Rafaella so that he knew what was happening. We climbed into the helicopter ready for take-off. When the helicopter lifted up, the views were simply amazing. It was incredible to by flying over St. Peter's and the Coliseum on the short flight down to Castel Gandolfo.

We soon touched down in the grounds of the Papal Palace at Castel Gandolfo. We thanked the pilot and then hurried off to Geno's family home. There was great activity and excitement in the house. We were met at the front door by Geno's mum, who had tears of joy streaming down her face. We were taken up to one of the bedrooms where Serena was resting and cuddling the most beautiful baby boy.

Geno embraced his sister and kissed the baby, with tears welling up in his eyes. We congratulated Serena and Stefano on their wonderful new arrival. Geno asked them if they had thought of any names just yet. "Well", explained Serena, "we're all really proud of you, Geno. The way that you have travelled and built a business is amazing. And it's really wonderful that you have been able to find happiness after your previous sadness. We would really like to call the baby 'Geno' if that's alright with you? And, of course, we would like you to be his godfather". Geno burst into tears of joy. "I would be so honoured", he said. Serena asked me if I would like to hold little Geno. "Thank you, love", I said, "but Geno isn't little, you know. Quite the opposite, in fact!" Then the penny dropped. "Oh, I'm sorry", I said; "You were talking about the baby, weren't you? Yes, I would love to hold him". I gently cuddled little Geno and held him tight. It's funny how you automatically start to sway gently and start singing lullabies when you hold a baby.

Amidst this happy scene, there was a knock on the front door. Dario went to answer it and returned a few moments later with a beautiful middle-aged woman with dark features and smouldering eyes. She said 'hello' to Geno. "Hello Magdalena", Geno replied. Magdalena congratulated Serena and Stefano on the safe arrival of their baby. "Thank you", they said, rather coldly. Geno introduced me to Magdalena: "This is Jim, my fiancé. Magdalena is an old, erm, friend of mine", Geno explained. "Just a friend am I!?", Magdalena exclaimed; "I thought I was rather more than that! I am the mother of your child after all!"

Chapter 9.

Saturday 26th December 2015.

Boxing Day.

I think I know why they call it Boxing Day. I wasn't prepared for the revelation that Geno has a child. It has sent me reeling. I know how these boxers must feel. I feel like I have had a pounding in the ring (not in a good way). There's nothing funny about getting a punch in the ring, believe me.

I love Geno so much. I just don't understand why he didn't feel able to tell me that he has a child. I thought that we were strong enough to tell each other anything. I don't know what I have done to make him think that he couldn't open up to me. I mean, he usually opens up for me quite a lot, let's be honest. And now he's gone off with Magdalena to talk things through. I hope they can sort things out. But I hope she doesn't want to get back with him. I would be devastated. What was it that Dolly Parton used to sing? 'You'd better keep your hands off my potential new boyfriend!' Ain't that the truth. Well, Geno is rather more than a potential new boyfriend. We are fiancés. Or at least we were. I don't know what we are now. I feel so alone. So far away from home. All I can do is sit here and twiddle with Geno's ring. I feel like that is all I have left of him.

Sunday 27th December 2015.

Geno came back late last night. We have had the chance to talk today. We went for a walk so that we could talk things through.

"I'm sorry, Jim", Geno began. "There is nothing to be sorry for", I said. "Are you angry with me Jim?"; he asked. "Oh Geno, I could never be angry with you. I don't want us to fight. Although I suppose it might be fun to exchange blows", I said; "I just don't understand why you didn't tell me, Geno. Did you think I wouldn't support you?" "Oh Jim", Geno continued, "it's just that I am a bit embarrassed. It's a bit unusual for a gay man to have a kid". "No, not at all", I said; "It's probably more common than you think. And being gay is no bar to having children, especially nowadays". "I suppose not", Geno said, "but I feel like such a failure. I feel like I've made a mistake". "Oh Geno, love, we've all made mistakes", I empathised; "Me more than most. But surely you don't see having a child as a mistake? I mean a child is a precious gift, a wonderful blessing". "Yes indeed", Geno agreed, "having children is wonderful, but I have not been able to be a very hands-on Dad, especially since I moved to England". "Well love, it's not too late", I said; "Let's see what we can do so that you can spend more time with your child".

"Can you tell me about your child, Geno?", I asked. "Well, she's beautiful", Geno began; "She's called Anna and she's 12 years old now". "Oh Geno, how wonderful to have a daughter!", I said; "You must be so proud of her". "Oh yes, she's wonderful", Geno beamed, "but I miss her so much. I'm so glad that we can talk about this, Jim. It's much better to have things out in the open. It has been weighing on my mind, like an awkward secret, like having a skeleton in my closet". "Oh mate, we've all got skeletons in our closets", I said; "I mean, I've got a whole flippin' graveyard in my closet, never mind a skeleton".

"I still don't understand, though, Geno, why didn't you tell me about Anna before now?", I asked. "Jim, it's difficult, you know", Geno explained; "You know what guys are like. It was hard for me to explain that I had married a woman and had a daughter. I was worried that you might think I was like a straight guy looking to experiment rather than a gay guy who was ready for a relationship". "Yes, I can understand that, Geno", I said, "but it is just part of life. We all have a past. And stereotypes are not very helpful. You shouldn't have to choose between being a father and being a gay man. You can have it all!"

As I reflected on Geno's comments, a wave of panic came over me momentarily. Well, there's no point panicking, so I thought I'd better have it out. "Geno, love", I said, "are you still married to Magdalena? Technically, I mean?" "No love", Geno replied; "I'm a divorced guy. I would never ask you to marry me if I wasn't free to do so". I smiled and breathed a sigh of relief. Thank goodness for that. I didn't want to be a pig in mist, after all.

"So, Geno", I went on, "can you tell me about how you met Magdalena?" "Ah yes. Magdalena and I are very old friends", Geno explained; "We go way back. We've known each other since school. Of course, I didn't really understand who I was back then. I just assumed that all the boys would grow up to marry girls, including myself. I didn't think there were any other paths to follow. Marriage seemed like a good idea. Magdalena and I got on so well and we genuinely loved each other. We were very sincere. We married for better and for worse". "Yes", I interjected, "you couldn't do any better, and poor Magdalena couldn't do any flippin' worse!"

"I'm sorry Geno", I said; "I know it's not a laughing matter. Please continue. If it's not too painful, can you tell me about how your marriage ended?" "Yes Jim", Geno said; "It would be good to talk about it and get it off my chest". "I wish you'd get that shirt off your chest!", I thought to myself, but fortunately, since we were having a serious conversation, I managed to not say it out loud. "We separated about 5 years ago", Geno explained; "Magdalena left to be with her new partner". "I'm sorry, love", I said; "Still I suppose that it's Magdalena's decision. It's her loss. And I know all about hair loss, believe me. It must have been hard, love". "Yes, it was", Geno said, "but we all get on well now. We are very old friends after all. And perhaps things happen for a reason. Perhaps Magdalena has done me a favour. As time has gone on, I feel like I have grown and been able to be more honest, open and true to myself. I mean, you know what it's like, Jim, when you have a heavy burden on your back". "Yes I do, mate", I said; "I really do".

"So Geno, please tell me, have you had romances with any other women?" "Oh no Jim", he replied; "I've only ever had one woman". "Right, mate", I said; "Are you bragging or complaining?!" "I'm certainly not complaining, Jim", he replied, "it's just that I have come to realise that I'm better suited to having a relationship with a guy". "Yes love, I know what you mean", I said; "Everything felt so right and natural with you. I used to feel so happy with you, so safe in your arms". "So Jim, do you still want to get married?", Geno asked. I hesitated for a moment. "Geno, I love you", I said; "Ever since I met you, you have put a song in my heart and a spring in my step. Well, not just my step, to be honest. But I wish you had told me about Anna. I think in a relationship it is important to have lots of trust, you know? Well, it's also good to have lots of thrust too". "So what are you saying, Jim?", Geno asked; "Do you just want to toss me aside?" "No Geno", I said; "Of course you know that I love to toss you off, but I certainly don't want to leave you. I just think we should take things slowly, and give ourselves a chance to think and reflect". "Fair enough, Jim", said Geno; "Let's just sleep on it and see what tomorrow brings".

Monday 28th December 2015.

I feel a lot better today, having spoken to Geno. I really hope that things work out for us. I really feel for Geno. It's like he has been carrying this secret around and it has been a burden to him, when really it needn't have been a secret at all. I'm just a bit worried. I wonder if there is anything else that he is keeping from me? I suppose we shouldn't rush into marriage. I guess we have only known each other for a few months. Let's just take it steady.

Fortunately, I have had some work to do today to keep me occupied and to keep my mind off things. I was supervising the installation of the new fire in the Sistine Chapel. They will only be using it every few years for the conclaves, so we opted for a lovely cast-iron wood-burning stove. There's no point in putting in a gas supply pipe if the fire is only going to be used infrequently. I can't imagine that the Pope would want me interfering with his plumbing in that way. I did manage to put in a special fan system, though, that pushes the smoke up the chimney so that it can really billow out on the roof. So have a look the next time they are electing a Pope – there should be plenty of white emissions. Oh my goodness, it sounds like I am talking about Geno again!

Tuesday 29th December 2015.

Well, the Pope seems to be very happy with his new fire in the Sistine Chapel. Now that it's been installed I've got a bit more time on my hands. Geno explained that he had been talking to Magdalena again about him spending a bit more time with Anna, and he asked me if I would like to spend the day taking Anna out. "Oh Geno, that would be wonderful to meet your daughter!", I said; "We could take her to the park, or shopping, or for lunch". "Yes, good ideas, Jim", Geno said; "Or perhaps we could go to the zoo. Anna really loves animals".

We went over to Magdalena's house to collect Anna. Anna was a beautiful young lady with long brown hair and lovely manners. She spoke really good English. We got organised and set out for the *Bioparco*, which apparently is the zoo in Rome. Anna loved seeing all the animals, especially the cute little pygmy hippos. She loved seeing the elephants. "Wow, this one's got a really long trunk!", she said. "Yeah, just like your Dad", I thought to myself. "Come on", said Geno, "there's a children's farm over this way, where the kids can meet smaller animals like rabbits and do some petting". "Hmm, not quite the type of petting I was hoping to do with you, Geno", I said, "but let's give it a go". We had a really great time at the zoo. I really enjoyed telling Anna all about the different animals. "You seem to know a lot", she said; "Will you come round and help me with my homework sometime?" Of course, I promised that I would.

Later on, back in town, Geno asked Anna if she would like to stop off for some tea. He spotted a Burger King and asked Anna and me if that would be OK. "Sure", I said, "although I must say, with you, Geno, I've already got a Whopper!".

As the afternoon gave way to evening, we safely delivered Anna back home. She said she had had a great day and would like to see more of her Dad. (I must admit, I've already seen all of him). As we travelled back to Castel Gandolfo, Geno was flashing, no, sorry, that doesn't sound right; Geno was beaming with joy at being reunited with his daughter. "How do you feel, love?", I asked. "Delighted to be spending time with Anna", he said; "But also worried. I mean what will happen when we go back to England? I'm going to lose Anna all over again". "No, not necessarily", I replied; "We'll find a way to make it work".

Wednesday 30th December 2015.

As promised, today Geno and I went over to Magdalena's house to help Anna with her homework which she needed to do over the school holidays. We found Anna in the kitchen making a little snack. She finished up and was taking her snack out of the kitchen into her room to start work. I reminded her to turn the light off in the kitchen. "We always turn the light off when we have finished in a room", I said, "otherwise, Lumie the Light Fairy gets very upset. Lumie does not like us to waste energy". Anna gave me a very puzzled look and said, "Don't be silly; there's no Light Fairy". "Of course there is, love", I replied; "Believe me, I know lots of fairies".

After Anna had eaten her snack, she settled down to work. We had a look at a Maths question first. Geno kindly translated the question for me: 'Donatella sits in her room playing with coloured buttons. She has 10 red buttons and 5 blue buttons in a bag. She takes one button out at random, but does not replace it. She then takes another button out at random and does not replace it. What is the probability that both of the buttons taken out were red?' Well, I was up in arms! I was outraged! To think that there was some poor girl locked in a bedroom somewhere with only a bag of buttons for company! Don't they have Social Services in Italy? Why hasn't someone called them? Honestly, it's like poor Anne Frank all over again. And why is the poor girl so disturbed that she has taken all the buttons off her clothes in the first place? Well, Geno reassured me that it was not a real girl and that it was just an exam question, so then I felt a bit better. I showed Anna how to draw a probability tree to work out the likelihood of getting the two red buttons. "And tell me, what is the probability of you marrying me, Jim?", Geno asked. "High, love", I replied; "Please just give me some time".

Next up was some research for a science project on evolution. I pulled up some facts about Charles Darwin on the computer, and made some notes about the different species he discovered on his travels. "Look, Anna", I said; "It says here that Charles Darwin travelled right around the world on the voyage of the *Beagle*. Imagine being able to sail across the whole world on a dog!" "No, I think that the *Beagle* was a ship", Anna explained. "Oh, right", I said; "Sorry, love. Well let's see if we can draw some pictures of the ship and of some of the animals he discovered so we can put them in the project. Geno, love, do you know if there are any coloured pencils or crayons about the place?" Geno managed to produce a set of colouring pencils from a cupboard. "Ah, thank you darling", I said; "Oh Geno, you're so well-equipped!" "Well, I haven't had any complaints", he replied.

Once the homework was finished, we kissed Anna goodbye and headed back to Castel Gandolfo. "Thank you so much for helping Anna with her work, Jim", Geno said. "It's no trouble, love; it was my pleasure", I said; "I want to make sure that all the homework gets done – I don't want to get into trouble with the teacher! I do hope you won't have to cane me, Geno!" "Well, love", Geno said, "I think I might have to give you a spot of detention this evening!" "Ooh yes please, baby, I've been a bad boy! I think I do need to be punished!" And with that we settled down and snuggled up for the evening.

Thursday 31st December 2015.

New Year's Eve!!!

I can't believe that the year is almost at an end! What an amazing year it has been! My life has just turned around since I met Geno. He has given me a whole new outlook on life. I just hope that I don't lose him now. I hope I can learn to trust him again.

Geno is taking me out tonight for a New Year's party at a karaoke bar! Luckily I have brought plenty of slap with me so I can try to make myself look presentable. I'd better get cracking...

••

We left the house at 8 p.m. to go over to the karaoke bar. Geno looked stunning with his dark hair swept back. I mean I had tried my best to style my hair too. Both of them. Geno was wearing a beautiful blue patterned shirt and a stunning jacket, and basically was looking even more attractive than usual. He seemed to have a radiant glow. I've warned him about going on them sunbeds. But seriously I think he was glowing from having seen Anna again. I think that fatherhood really agrees with him.

We arrived at the bar at about 8.30 p.m. and Geno ordered some drinks. "I feel like a wine tonight", Geno said. "That's not like you, love", I said; "I've never heard you complain or whine about anything. Mind you, I must admit that I do like to hear you moan". "No Jim", Geno said, "I mean I'd like to have a glass of wine. What would you like?" "Oh, just a blackcurrant and soda for me please", I replied. "Are you sure you wouldn't like something hard to drink?", Geno asked. "Well yes, love, of course", I replied, "but not in public". "Oh Jim", Geno said, "I meant, do you want an alcoholic drink?" "Oh no, thank you, love", I replied; "It goes straight to my head! One sip and I'll be anybody's! Or more likely I'll be nobody's, knowing my luck!"

We sipped our drinks and then went over to the dance floor and the DJ's booth to choose a song to sing. "Let's have a bit of Abba!", Geno suggested. "Fab!", I agreed; "Now you're talking". I was so excited as the intro blasted out, and then I heard Geno belting it out: "Gimme, gimme, gimme, a man after midnight!" "When did you become so picky and particular?", I asked; "Insisting on a man after midnight, indeed! From what I remember, you were more than happy to have men before midnight, after midnight, on the flippin' stroke of midnight..." Geno ignored me and carried on: "Won't somebody help me chase the shadows away?" "Why do you need to chase The Shadows away, love?", I asked; "What has Cliff Richard ever done to you?"

After we had finished singing, we went to have another little drink. It was getting busier in the bar (despite our singing!) but Geno managed to get us a couple of stools to sit on. "Are you OK sitting on these bar stools, love?", he asked. "Oh yes love", I said, "after all, I've sat on worse things than that over the years, let's be honest".

It was a wonderful evening; we danced and sang and laughed. It was like being back with the old Geno that I knew and loved. I really hope that things work out for us. Maybe 2016 will be a great year for us. I hope so. As midnight approached, we all got ready to welcome in the new year, with the traditional countdown: *"Dieci, nove, otto, sette, sei, cinque, quattro, tre, due, uno, Felice anno nuovo!"* As the fireworks began, I kissed Geno and held him tight as we saw the New Year in together.

Friday 1ˢᵗ January 2016.

New Year's Day!! Happy New Year to you!! *Felice anno nuovo!*

I dread to think what time we woke up today. I was in a terrible state. I wouldn't mind but I don't even drink. It seems like even soft drinks go straight to my head. Geno wasn't much better, but he managed to get up and make a pot of coffee before coming back to bed.

"Would you like something strong and steamy?", Geno asked as he poured me a cup; "Cream and sugar?" "Yes please angel", I replied; "I'll give it a go". Well, after I had tasted Geno's hot cream, we settled down and snuggled up. "Happy new year, Geno!", I said. "Happy new year to you, Jim", he replied; "I hope that 2016 will be a great year for us". "Yes, Geno", I said, "I really hope so".

"Jim, may I say something?", Geno asked. "Yes of course, love", I replied; "Anything". "I love you Jim", Geno went on; "I want to be with you. Do you love me?" "Oh Geno", I replied, "you know that I love you. I adore you. You are the only man for me". "So, will you marry me, Jim?", Geno asked. I hesitated. "Geno, I just think we need some time to think", I said; "Let's not rush into anything". "Are you still angry with me, Jim?", Geno asked. "No, love, of course not", I replied; "I was never angry with you. I simply couldn't be angry with you. I love you, and so I wish you had felt you were able to talk to me about anything. I mean, is there anything else you haven't told me which I should know about?" Geno thought for a moment. "Well, I am kind of into cling film in a big way", he said. "Oh, right", I said; "Well, I suppose that is to be expected when you work in catering. And it could really spice up our trips to the Home and Bargain". "I'm sorry that I didn't tell you about Anna and Magdalena sooner, Jim", Geno said. "It's OK", I said; "It's just that I thought you were the perfect man. I didn't think that you would have any secrets. I suppose I was a bit disappointed when I discovered that you were human, after all. In fact, I haven't been that disappointed since the time I queued up outside Dorothy Perkins because the poster said they were having a sale on versatile tops and bottoms".

"Well, love, we're all human", Geno said; "No-one's perfect. But that's no reason to give up on our relationship. Let's give it a go". "Yes, darling", I agreed; "You're the best. I can't think of anyone else that I'd rather be with". I kissed Geno and held him tight. "Let's have a little siesta", he said. "Oh no, love", I replied, "that was quite a New Year's party last night; I couldn't manage a fiesta now". "No love", Geno explained, "I mean let's have a little snooze before we get up. We've got a lot to do later getting packed and organised ready for our flight back to England tomorrow". So we snuggled up, and happily fell asleep in one another's arms.

Saturday 2nd January 2016.

We got up early to finish packing and to say our goodbyes to Geno's family. I couldn't thank them enough for their kind hospitality and helping me to enjoy my first Italian adventure. After breakfast, we collected our bags together and packed them into Dario's car as he was kindly taking us to the airport.

Dario drove us firstly over to Magdalena's house so that we could say goodbye to Anna. Both Anna and Geno were very tearful and emotional, but Geno promised that he would visit again as soon as possible. After we had said our goodbyes, Dario drove us over to the airport.

On arrival at the airport, Geno and I hugged Dario and thanked him for the lift. "Please could you get me a trolley for this luggage, baby?", Geno asked me. "Certainly, hun", I replied; "Although I must admit, I thought that getting trolleyed was more your sort of thing, Geno".

We loaded up the trolley and trundled into the airport building to check in. We checked our bags in and then leisurely strolled over to a café as there was plenty of time before the plane departed. "So, we'll soon be on our way back to England", Geno said; "Tell me Jim, are you ready for take-off?" "Certainly, love", I replied; "What would you like me to take off first?"

We went to the counter in the café to order a pot of tea. Geno chose a beautiful cake too. "Oh, you want to be careful with those cakes, baby", I said; "You don't want to put on weight". "Are you suggesting that I'm fat, Jim?", Geno asked indignantly; "I'll have you know that I've got a perfect BMI". "A perfect BMI?", I queried; "Geno, I didn't even know you had a car".

We settled down in the café to have a little sip of tea, but our relaxation was disturbed and we were startled to hear our names called out over the tannoy: "Please would passengers James Fitzgerald and Geno Aquinta return to the check-in desk for an urgent message".

Chapter 10.

Saturday 2nd January 2016 (continued).

Geno and I ran back to the check-in desk, hoping and praying that no-one was sick or hurt. The clerk handed Geno a note which was a message from Magdalena asking Geno to phone her urgently. We panicked and worried that Anna might have had an accident, but when Geno dialled and got through to Magdalena, she assured him that Anna was safe and well. Anna was, however, very upset.

It turned out that Anna had become very upset about seeing her Dad leave and really wanted to see him again before he left Italy. Magdalena was asking Geno if she could bring Anna over to the airport to see Geno. There was a good 90 minutes before we had to be at the departure gate, so Geno said that would be great. Magdalena said that she would be right over.

After finishing the phone call, Geno said: "Oh Jim, I don't know whether I've done the right thing. I wonder if Anna will be more upset having to say goodbye to me a second time here at the airport". "Well", I said; "Anna is a clever young lady; she knows her own mind. She just wants to spend a bit more time with her Dad".

Shortly, Magdalena and Anna arrived, running into the airport building. Anna ran straight into Geno's arms, and as he hugged her, he lifted her up and spun her around. "Do you have to go, Dad?", Anna begged; "It's been fun having you back. I really enjoyed going out to the zoo. And I like you too, Jim, you're great at homework!" "Oh, baby", Geno said, "I'll be back as soon as I can, it's just that I have to sort some things out in England. But I'll come back to visit you as much as I can".

Anna looked very sad. Eventually she said, "Why can't I come and stay with you in England for a bit?" "Oh Anna, darling", Geno said, "I will arrange for you to come over in the holidays, but it's not sensible to come just now. You'll have your new term at school starting soon, and both Jim and I are working all the time, I would worry that we wouldn't be able to look after you properly". "I'm 12, Dad!", Anna said, "I don't need anyone to look after me!" "Well, angel", Geno continued, "even when you are a big 12 you still need someone to help you sometimes".

As there was plenty of time before the plane was due to depart, I suggested that we all go over to the café so everyone could have a proper chat. As we walked over to the café, I had a quiet word with Geno: "Geno, this could be a wonderful opportunity for you to spend more time with your daughter. Anna clearly adores you". "I'm not sure if it's a good idea, Jim", he replied; "I mean, you know how busy we both are; like I said I am worried that I wouldn't be able to look after her properly". "Oh Geno, I'm sure you would be able to look after her perfectly", I said; "You know that I will help as much as possible. And I'm sure she would enjoy helping you and Lucy in the café. I think Anna would be delighted to go around with you in the ice cream van – it would be a child's dream! And, of course, I'm sure she will love Clara – I don't think Anna has any pets of her own at the moment". "Oh Jim, I'm not sure", Geno said; "I mean, the school term will be starting again very shortly". "Well, love, if Anna wants to stay for a few weeks", I said, "we could speak to some of the local schools to see if they could take her as a temporary student". "Well, maybe", Geno conceded. "Sure, baby", I said; "I mean you have a spare room at the flat, so why ever not?" "Yes, you're right", Geno said, "I'll talk to Magdalena".

Geno and Magdalena sat at one table for a quiet chat while I took Anna to get a milkshake. I told Anna not to worry and that her Mum and Dad would work something out. Eventually, Geno and Magdalena came over. Geno had clearly managed to reassure Magdalena that Anna would be OK, as she came over and asked Anna if she would like to go to England for a couple of weeks. "Oh yes!", she said, as she gave both her Mum and Dad a big hug.

"So, when will Anna be coming over to England?", Geno asked. "I'll try to arrange a flight in the next few days", Magdalena suggested. "Well how about now?", Anna said. "Oh, don't be silly, darling", Magdalena said; "We'll have to pack some clothes. And you can't travel without your passport". "I already have my passport", Anna said, producing it from her coat pocket; "And I have already packed some clothes. I packed a case and it's in the trunk of the car". "Wow, you go girl!", I said; "I told you that she was a young lady who knows what she wants, Geno". "Well, I suppose that there is no time like the present", Geno said. Magdalena took Anna back to the car park to pick up her case from the car, while Geno and I raced over to the ticket desk to see if there was any chance of buying an extra ticket for our flight. We were lucky, very lucky, in managing to get one of the few remaining seats.

As Anna and Magdalena walked back in to the airport building, Geno smiled a victorious grin and took great pleasure in telling Anna that she had a seat on the plane to Manchester. Anna was so excited, she kissed and hugged her Dad, then said goodbye to her Mum. We promised to phone Magdalena as soon as we got home. Then it was time to check Anna's case in and go through passport control before going to the departure gate. Time was pressing a bit now and we had to run to make the flight. I found it hard to keep up with Anna and Geno. "Come on, Jim", Geno said; "Are you OK?" "Oh yes, love ", I replied; "Don't worry about me; I'm just coming up the rear".

Finally, we were able to take our seats on the plane and jet off back to Manchester.

Sunday 3rd January 2016.

Ah, it's good to be home. We got back last night, and it was lovely just to have a cup of tea in the flat. Clara was delighted to see us again and, as expected, Anna fell in love with the cat instantly.

You know, word has already started to get round about our engagement after Geno had posted the news on Facebook. When we got home there had already been some cards posted to the flat. Our friends had sent us some beautiful engagement cards; one in particular struck me – it had two elephants on the front with their trunks entwined. "Wow, Geno, they really do know us well!", I had said at the time. As I've mentioned before, Geno certainly has got a big trunk. Another card read: 'Congratulations on your engagement! You make the perfect couple!' A perfect couple of what, though, I really don't know.

As, of course, we had not been expecting to have a guest staying in the flat, the spare room was not quite ready. Well, not at all ready, really, because it did not contain a bed. Last night we had to improvise by using blankets and cushions to make Anna comfortable on the sofa. So, the first priority today was to nip to Argos to get another air bed. We climbed into the ice cream van and drove down to Bootle to pick one up. "Just look at this!", I said to Geno as I read him the product description from the catalogue, "Automatic inflation and deflation! It's like our air bed, Geno; the motor is so versatile – it can suck and blow! Fantastic!"

We loaded the airbed, duvet and bed linen into the ice cream van, and headed off for home, confident that Anna would be more comfortable and settled now. The rest of the afternoon was lovely; Anna loved visiting the park, the beach and the sand dunes. By the time evening came, Anna was shattered and keen to have an early night, so we made her a quick tea and then we set up the airbed and got her room organised.

Once Anna was settled for the night, Geno and I had a little bite. We had a little bit of supper too. "I think it would be a good idea for us to have an early night too, love", I said; "After all, we are back to work tomorrow". "Yes, angel", Geno agreed, "good thinking". So we quickly got ready for bed and hit the sack. That didn't half bring tears to my eyes.

The airbed didn't feel as sturdy as I remembered before we went to Italy. I was sure it had deflated a little bit while we had been away, but we took a chance, jumped into bed and drifted off to sleep. Well, the air must have kept on coming out, because we found ourselves rolling around on the floor in the middle of the night (not in a good way, I'm afraid). "This flippin' airbed is on the blink again!", I exclaimed. "Don't worry", said Geno, "I'll make it big again". "I wish", I said. Geno plugged in the airbed and tried to get it onto the inflate setting. "It's no good, Jim", he said, fiddling about with the controls; "This knob feels awfully stiff". "Surely, that's normally a good thing?", I joked. "Not in this case", Geno replied. "Well, let me have a go", I said. I must have been a bit heavy handed because a few seconds later I had to exclaim: "Oh Geno, I've pulled my knob off!"

Luckily I managed to get the knob back into position on its shaft and turn it to the inflate setting. But as soon as the air went in, it came out again just as fast. "Oh, no, Geno", I said, "it must have a puncture!" Well, try as we might, we could not find where the puncture was, so we gave up. You know what it's like; sometimes it's difficult to find a small prick. Fortunately Geno managed to dig a couple of old camping mats out of the cupboard. "Let's lay these mats down next to each other and then we can snuggle up", Geno said. "Good idea, Geno", I replied; "Just be careful you don't fall down the gap between the two mats; I don't want you falling down the crack. Mind you, you're very welcome to fall down my crack any time!"

Eventually we managed to get back to sleep. Airbeds, honestly, don't talk to me about flippin' airbeds!

Monday 4th January 2016.

Back to work today. What a busy day after Christmas! So busy and so much to catch up with! And so many engagement congratulations from my friends!

In the afternoon, when things had quietened down a bit, the boss asked me to train some of my colleagues up on the use of pyrolytic ovens. You know, I'm not sure they needed the training because I've seen them out on a Friday night and they already looked pretty pyrolytic to me.

After work, I went to catch up with my good friend, Vin, for coffee and tea. "Happy new year to you!", Vin said; "Tell me, Jim, what did you think of Rome?" "Oh, it was wonderful", I replied; "I loved it; there is just history everywhere". "And how is Geno?", Vin asked. I hesitated before answering. "Erm, have you read anything about us on Facebook, Vin?", I asked. "No, mate", he replied, "I haven't really been looking at Facebook. Why do you ask? Is everything OK?"

I took a deep breath. "Well, Vin", I began, "while we were in Rome, Geno proposed to me". "I bet he did!", Vin said; "I thought he looked like the type who might proposition you!" "No, mate", I explained; "I mean he asked me to marry him. In the dome of St. Peter's". "Oh I see!", Vin said; "And at St. Peter's Basilica! How romantic! You know, when my fiancé proposed to me, I had to make do with flippin' Berry Street in Chinatown!"

I smiled. "So tell me, Jim", Vin asked, "did you say 'yes'?" "Yes I did", I replied; "I love him, Vin; I want to spend my life with him". "Great", Vin said, but then he saw my troubled face; "So what's the problem then?" "Well", I explained, "Geno hadn't been entirely honest with me. I found out that Geno has a daughter from a previous marriage. I don't know what to do". "Ah, Jim", he said as he hugged me, "you know that we all have a past. Perhaps he was just waiting for the right time to tell you. Perhaps once you've had the chance to meet Geno's daughter you might feel calmer about the situation". "Oh, I have met her, Vin", I explained; "In fact, she is staying with us at the moment. She's called Anna, and she's lovely. She's so kind, caring and helpful; and she works hard at school". "Well, that all sounds very positive", Vin said; "It sounds like you get on well with Anna and that you're fond of her, so I really don't see a problem. OK, so perhaps Geno should have told you about her earlier on, but at least you have met her now. Jim, if you and Geno love each other, then you shouldn't let anything stop you being together. An opportunity like this may only come along once in a lifetime". "Yes, Vin", I said, "you're right. You're so right. You're so wise".

"And in any case", Vin continued, "I'm sure that Anna would love to be a bridesmaid!" "Oh, a bridesmaid, I hadn't really thought about that", I said; "I mean, it's not as if we are having any brides! Perhaps she could be a 'groomsmaid' instead! I think we might just have invented a new word there! Blimey, these same-sex weddings are really confusing. I can just imagine an usher welcoming guests and asking 'Are you a friend of the groom, or a friend of the other groom?'!" "Oh, don't worry about that", Vin said; "Just tell people to sit anywhere! But, you know, if Anna does want to be a 'groomsmaid' then I know a wonderful seamstress who can make beautiful dresses. She's even exhibited in Paris!" "Well, Vin", I said, "I've made an exhibition of myself in Paris once or twice too, let's be honest".

"And you know, I would love to play the violin at your wedding", Vin said. "Oh, yes, mate, that would be great", I said; "You are a wonderful fiddler! Do you think you could make a softer sound for a more romantic tune?" "Oh yes, certainly", Vin said; "I mean, if necessary, I can always pluck it". "Vin!", I exclaimed; "Honestly, I have never heard you use that sort of language!"

I was so grateful to Vin for helping me to see things clearly. As the evening drew to a close I asked Vin if he wanted any more coffee before we went home. "Oh no, mate, thank you", he said; "I've had my fill". "Oh, have you indeed!", I said; "And who is this Phil you've been having?!"

Tuesday 5th January 2016.

After work, Geno suggested that we take Anna to have a look around Liverpool One. As we walked around, Geno asked Anna if she would like to visit the Disney Store. I must admit, I felt a little bit awkward going in there. "Come on, Jim", Geno said; "It will be fun! We can pretend to be princesses. I'll be Snow White, and you can be Cinderella!" "Don't be daft", I replied; "I can't be Cinderella! I mean honestly, Geno, have you ever known me to run away from balls?"

So we went into the Disney Store and Anna had a good look round. Anna was very taken by this little set of erasers shaped like snowmen, so Geno bought them for her. "What do you think of these?", Geno asked me. "They're lovely, angel", I replied, "and they make a change from the type of rubbers that you normally buy".

After we had had a look around the shops, Geno suggested that we go for a little bite to eat. "Good idea", I said to Geno; "It's always good to find something to fill a hole". We saw a new burger place in town called 'Five Guys'. "Shall we give this place a try?", Geno asked. "Oh, no, Geno, please", I said; "I can barely handle one guy, never mind five guys!" "Well, let's go into this coffee shop instead", Geno said; "You know, they've got a really cute barista!" "A barrister!?", I exclaimed; "Oh, Geno, you're not in trouble with the law, are you?" "No, love", Geno replied, "not a barrister, a barista; he's very good at grinding his beans". Well, that sounded very promising, so in we went!

Inside the coffee shop, Anna chose a hot chocolate and a chocolate brownie. "Why don't you have a chocolate girl guide instead, love?", I suggested; "It might be a bit bigger!" Geno said: "I think I'll have a fruit daiquiri". "Oh aye", I said, "and who is this Zachary that you are carrying on with?! I'm sure he is a sweet fruit, but let's be honest, Geno, you've had more fruits over the years than the flippin' harvest festival!"

Geno, ignored me and tried to put the conversation on a different track. "How about you, Jim", he said, "would you like a sticky bun?" "Well, love", I replied, "I do like it when you make my buns sticky!" "Or they are doing some hot food", Geno continued; "Would you like a vegetarian nut roast?" "Oh Geno", I said, "you can roast my nuts any time you like!"

After tea, we got the train back to Crosby. Anna was tired and so we arranged to get a taxi from the station back to the flat. Geno asked me: "Jim, do you mind going in the back of the taxi?" "Not at all, love", I replied; "You know that I much prefer it in the back".

Wednesday 6th January 2016.

Anna was keen to stay in England for longer, so Geno started making enquiries about enrolling her in a school. "What is the name of that good school up on the hill?", Geno asked; "I think I will go up and ask if they have any vacancies. Yes, I'll pop up to Mount Vernon". "Never mind Vernon!", I replied; "I wish you would mount me!"

But seriously, though, Geno is taking Anna's education very seriously. He has even bought her a computer thing to help with homework. He calls it a big Mac. I didn't even know that McDonalds did computers.

Saturday 9th January 2016.

I was aroused very early this morning. There was drilling and banging and knocking (not in a good way). I think there were some noisy builders doing some work in one of the flats downstairs. Honestly, you would think I would be used to having fellas pounding away downstairs by now.

I went into the kitchen to find Geno and Anna singing away to the radio. Anna has a lovely singing voice; Geno, well, perhaps a little less so. "What do you think, Jim?", Geno asked; "We could start a group, like the Von Trapp family singers". "Well, maybe, love", I said; "Although with your singing, Geno, people might rename it 'the Shut Your Trap family singers'!" Anna rolled her eyes and took her cereal into the lounge. "Well, Jim", Geno went on, "perhaps we could cut a demo and start a boy-band instead?" "Well", I hesitated, "I suppose that anything is possible. What would you call the band?" "Well, love", Geno replied, "if you are in it, I think we should call it 'One Cute Butt'!" I laughed. "Thank you, darling", I said, as I kissed him.

"I love having Anna staying with us", Geno said; "It's hard though, you know, juggling work and taking her to school. It's like we're always on the go; always chasing our tails". "Well, Geno", I said, "I do love chasing your tail!" "I hope that Anna stays for a while", Geno said; "I'd really like to take her to see Adele in March". "A Dell?", I asked; "But I thought Anna already had a computer?" "Well", continued Geno, "perhaps I will take Anna to see the pre-Raphaelites exhibition at the art gallery". "Wow, you're very cultured, Geno!", I said; "I'm lucky if I get to see a flippin' traffic light".

"So, tell me Jim", Geno asked, "are you still writing your diary?" "Oh, yes, love", I replied; "Of course. I like to record my thoughts and the day's events". "Well", said Geno, "I think it would be fun if someone made a film version of it sometime!" "Maybe, love", I replied; "Perhaps one day we will be immortalised in cellulite". "And what would the title be?", asked Geno; "Will it be more like '50 Shades of

Gay' or will it be more like 'My Big Fat Gay Wedding'?" "Oh, we'll see, love", I replied.

"Jim", Geno said; "It is wonderful that I am reconciled with my daughter, but I need one more thing to make my life complete. I love you. I want to spend my life with you. There is so much more of Italy that I would like to show you. I know this beautiful town called Lucca that we could visit". "That sounds very appropriate", I said; "After all, Geno, you are a very good-looker!" "Or perhaps we could travel further afield?", Geno suggested; "I mean, how do you feel about Bangkok?" "Oh, no, love", I said, "that sounds very painful".

"Why are you talking so much about the future, Geno?", I asked. "Oh Jim", he replied, "I wanted to ask you again. I love you, I adore you. Please have you had a chance to think? Please, do you feel that you could marry me?" I took a deep breath, then answered simply: "I do".

We kissed. I felt giddy. "Oh Geno", I said, "I don't know what has come over me!" "Come on", he said, "let's go and tell Anna the good news!"

The End.

(Well, for now, like; but don't get too comfortable!)

Printed in Great Britain
by Amazon

13155059R00086